The Awkward Autumn of Lily McLean

Lindsay Littleson

Kelpies

The Awkward Autumn of Lily McLean

L

'Gl
Lit
na

Kelpies is an imprint of Floris Books
First published in 2017 by Floris Books
© 2017 Lindsay Littleson

Lindsay Littleson has asserted her right under the
Copyright, Designs and Patent Act 1988 to be
identified as the Author of this work

This publisher acknowledges subsidy from
Creative Scotland towards the publication
of this volume

 Also available as an eBook

British Library CIP data available
ISBN 978-178250-354-5
Printed in Poland

To my sister Lesley,
with lots and lots of love.

Chapter 1

Things that could go wrong at high school:

- The work might be too hard. Maths lessons can only get worse.
- All the teachers might hate me. I'm Jenna's little sister, after all.
- Bullies might stick my head down the toilet. (Jenna told me that happened once, to someone who knows someone she knows.)
- I could get lost in the corridors.

"Help!" I whisper, pulling the duvet over my head.

I feel a jolt of sheer terror, the kind of gut-wrenching fear you experience at the top of a rollercoaster, knowing you're about to plummet to earth and you can't get off (well, you could get off, but it would make things worse). Nobody can help. It's happening. I'm starting high school today.

I know this isn't exactly positive thinking, but it's no wonder I'm feeling anxious. A lot went wrong at the end of primary school: I thought I was going crazy hearing and seeing things (it's a long story); I nearly drowned while on holiday with my gran and my best friends; and then my baby sister *sort of* saved my life (like I said, it's a long story).

I get up about three hours too early and put on my new uniform.

I use the word 'new' loosely – most of it once belonged to Jenna, except for the clunky black shoes. Mum bought those especially for me, from the charity shop in Largs' Main Street. I'm very worried that someone at school will recognise them as their old cast-offs. That would be just my luck.

When I eventually creep downstairs, Mum's in the kitchen doling out jammy toast to baby Summer and my wee brothers Bronx and Hudson. No sign of Jenna – she'll be in the bathroom putting on extra eyeliner.

"Oh, you look lovely, Lily! So smart. Doesn't she look great, boys?" trills Mum.

My wee brothers gawp at me, their jam-smeared mouths wide open.

"You look funny, Lil," says Bronx, spraying toast crumbs.

"Thanks. Looking forward to going back to school, lads?"

Hudson pulls a face. "I'm not going. I've got a sore tummy." He clutches his stomach and groans, unconvincingly.

"Rubbish!" Mum has a panicky note in her voice. "You're perfectly fine. You've just demolished three slices of toast."

"The toast's given me a sore tummy," insists Hudson, his lip wobbling, grey eyes filling with tears.

"Wiwy!" Summer bangs her spoon on her highchair, desperate for attention. "Let's go ducks!"

She grins at me. There's jam smeared all over her chin. It's hard to believe she saved my life the night I nearly drowned. Of course, she wasn't a baby when she did it. It still doesn't make sense in my head, but it happened.

"Sorry, Summer," I stammer. "We can't go and feed the ducks this morning. I've got to go to school."

"Yes, and I've got to get to work," says Mum, searching for her bag. "I thought your gran would be here by now."

Right on cue, the doorbell rings.

Gran fills the doorway, her beige quilted raincoat making her look even larger than usual.

"Lily, your tie's squint." She marches in and dumps her big shiny handbag down on the worktop. "And you'll need to run a comb through that hair before you go. Look at the state of this kitchen. Has nobody washed a dish since I was here last?"

Mum turns her back so Gran doesn't spot her rolling her eyes. She grabs her bag from where she'd abandoned it last night, wedged between the bin and the cats' bowls.

"Thanks for coming round, Morag. I'll leave you to it." Mum stops by the door, points at Hudson and mouths: "He's faking."

Gran nods and narrows her eyes at Hudson. He's got no hope of skipping school now.

"Be good for your gran, you three," trills Mum, before shouting Jenna's name up the stairs and turning, at last, to me. "Come on, Lily. You'd better get going too."

I check that I've attached my water lily charm to my schoolbag; I'll need some good luck today. Just as I'm about to follow Mum out the door, Jenna slopes into the kitchen, takes one look at me and bursts out laughing.

"I'd forgotten it's your first day! I'll pretend I don't know you – it'll be better for both of us. Watch out for Mr Diarmid. He's evil."

She sweeps out ahead of me, banging the door behind her.

Thanks, Jenna. I feel so much better now.

My feet, in their clumsy black shoes, drag as I head along the pavement towards Moorburn High. As promised, my big sister has left me to walk alone, but when I turn the corner, I see David, Aisha and Rowan waiting for me at the school gate, and I feel lighter.

"Hi Lily!" shrieks Aisha, waving both hands, eyes bright with excitement. Her short black bob gleams like silk in the sun.

Rowan is waving too, and bouncing up and down on the spot. Her nut-brown curls are tied back in a neat ponytail.

I run my hand through my own lank red hair, trying to make myself look a bit tidier. Gran was right: I should have combed it this morning and I know it needs washed. 'When the genes were shared out,' Gran always says, 'Jenna got the shiny blonde hair and Lily got the common sense.' Mum gets mad at her every time she says that, but I wonder if maybe Gran is right. Jenna has since dyed her lovely blonde hair black with purple streaks, which proves her point really.

"Hi, Lil. Bet you're not as terrified as me," David calls me over.

At least Dave won't notice what I'm wearing. He would only show an interest in my clothes if I arrived at school dressed as a Wookie or a Stormtrooper. He's as scruffy as he was at primary school: shirt hanging out of his trousers, wire glasses perched lopsidedly on his freckled nose, sandy hair sticking out in all directions. He makes me feel less conscious that my blazer is two sizes too big and my tights are laddered at the knee. Aisha and Rowan look super smart in their black skirts and school blazers. Their shoes are shiny and their black tights look new. I watch the two girls laughing together and feel suddenly like the odd one out, even though Rowan and I have been friends since nursery school.

"Hi, Lily. Love your shoes. Very retro," says Rowan, staring down at her own shiny shoes. "Mine are hideous. Mum and I had such a fight in Clarks. She forgets I'm not three any more. If she had her way I'd be wearing the ones with a wee toy hidden in the heel."

"My mum's the same. She's a total frump," sighs Aisha. "You're lucky, Lily. Your mum wears really unusual stuff. And she was so nice when we turned up in her café during the holidays."

"Yeah, it was a good day – though it's not Mum's café. She works there part-time," I say, anxious in case Aisha thinks we can cadge free drinks and sweets on a regular basis. That was definitely a one-off. The strawberry sundaes were delicious though, and Aisha had clearly been impressed, so it was worth the telling off I got from Mum afterwards.

A tall, balding man in a suit appears at the front gate.

"That's Mr Diarmid, the Depute Head," hisses Rowan. "I've heard he's fierce."

Mr Diarmid ignores us and gestures at a skinny teenager in a grey hoodie lurking by the gate. "Right, Dixon. Off you go. You're no longer on the school roll, so don't hang around the gate."

The lad swears, spits on the ground. "Tell Connor Murray he's for it."

Mr Diarmid strides over.

"If you come round here again, spoiling for a fight, Kai Dixon, I'll call the police." Mr Diarmid towers over the boy. "Scarper!"

Kai Dixon notices us staring at him, spits again and slopes off. When he's a safe distance from Mr Diarmid, he turns round and yells: "I'll go wherever I flamin' well like! You'd better watch your back, Diarmid!"

Then he breaks into a run, heading down the hill towards the shore.

"He's a right charmer," murmurs David. "Bet they didn't put *his* photograph on the cover of the school handbook."

"I've heard that name before. Kai was in my brother's year," whispers Aisha, "but he was expelled for fighting. Imran says he's a thief too. Nobody's phone was safe when Kai was around."

"Bell's about to ring! First years to the hall!" calls Mr Diarmid. "Come on, you sorry-looking lot. Get moving or there'll be trouble!"

"Do you think Mr Diarmid used to be in the army?" whispers Rowan as he marches us into the building.

He steers us towards the hall and we pass my sister, who's hanging around the lockers with her friends. As promised, she pretends she doesn't know me, which turns out to be a good thing.

"Jenna McLean! Get that chewing gum out of your mouth!" roars Mr Diarmid. "You know perfectly well it's against school rules! I do not want to see you in detention this term, do you hear me?"

I don't wait around to hear Jenna's reply.

I feel more and more overwhelmed as I stand, awkward and nervous, in the hall, trying to listen to a zillion instructions from our new teachers. There are some faces here I recognise from primary, but there are also loads of strangers. How on earth am I going to learn all their names?

"That's Danielle, Georgia and Jade," I whisper to Aisha, remembering that she must recognise hardly anyone, because she went to primary school on Cumbrae. David, Rowan and I have been friends since we were tiny; we only met Aisha on our holiday this summer. "Georgia and Rowan are neighbours and they're all in the netball team, so Rowan's included in their gang, but all of them except Rowan do their best not to acknowledge my existence. You might have more luck."

Georgia is tossing her long blonde hair back and forth as she giggles with her friends. There's a commotion going on behind her.

"Oh, and that's Big Cheryl, headbutting that boy," I add.

"Why's she called Big Cheryl?" asks Aisha, with a puzzled frown. "She's not very big."

"There used to be another Cheryl in our class," explains Rowan. "She was tiny, so we called them Big Cheryl and Wee Cheryl. And even when Wee Cheryl left, Big Cheryl's nickname stuck."

"Lucky Cheryl," murmurs Aisha.

"That's Doug the Thug over there," points David. "His nickname won't be a mystery for long, though he's an angel compared to that Kai Dixon."

"Lockers are allocated on a first come, first served basis," announces Mr Diarmid. "If you wish one, collect a form on your way out."

As he's speaking, I become aware of whispering behind me.

"See that girl over there? Her photo was in the papers!"

"What did she do?"

"Fell off Millport pier and nearly drowned!"

I flush red. They must have read all about what happened during the summer. Even people who don't know me know something about me. It's a horrible thought.

David must have heard the whispers too.

"You're The Girl Who Lived." He grins.

Mr Diarmid's still speaking.

"You will also be handed a timetable and a school map. It is your responsibility to make sure you're in the right classes at the correct times."

That sounds easy, but it isn't at first. The high school's massive – a maze of corridors and zigzagging staircases leading to different floors, like one of those very complicated hamster cages.

I glance at my timetable and see that my class's first proper lesson is P.E. Not a great start. Before I know it I'm standing in a massive gym hall lined with devices that look like instruments of torture.

Miss Swanage, our gym teacher, uses her whistle too often for my liking. She orders us to run round and round the gym and watches us with a smirk. I resolve to avoid P.E. as much as possible in future.

"This is not fun," I pant, as I stumble past the basketball hoops for the umpteenth time. "Aren't teachers meant to think up interesting and engaging lessons?"

"She's testing our fitness!" yells Rowan, racing past me. "Keep up, Lil and Dave! You too, Aisha!"

"I think I'm about to keel over and die," gasps David. "My lungs are actually bursting."

Rowan laps us yet again, waving her arms like a cheerleader who's lost her pompoms.

"You can do it, you three!"

"No, we really can't," groans Aisha. "We're done for."

I lag behind, as do Aisha and David. I think we might have just failed the surprise fitness test. Miss Swanage blows her whistle so loudly I fear for my eardrums.

Up next is English class. Mr Barton is very nice and smiley. He doesn't use a whistle once and he says we'll be reading *War Horse* and we might get to watch the National Theatre film version at the end of term, if we behave ourselves. I think Mr Barton must have spent longer at teacher training college than Miss Swanage.

David insists I sit next to him to help him avoid the horror of being Doug the Thug's shoulder partner, and Rowan and Aisha sit behind us. Aisha jokes around in English class, making everybody laugh (including Mr Barton). It's really good to see how well she gets on with my other friends. She does go a bit far though.

"Loving Mr Barton's corduroy jacket," she giggles, too loudly. "Very fashionable. Not."

He frowns and wags a finger at her.

"We're discussing this term's set texts, Aisha. If you prefer to chat about my jacket, which is vintage, incidentally, you can do it during detention."

By the end of the first day at high school, I'm feeling shattered but quietly relieved. Nothing terrible happened, most of the teachers seemed human and I enjoyed spending time with my friends. I don't know why I was so worried.

When I get home, Mum's still at work so Gran's in the kitchen, stirring soup. Jenna's out, Hudson and Bronx are watching cartoons in the living room and Summer's having a nap. Everything's peaceful.

Of course the peace doesn't last five minutes. I've just made myself a cup of tea when Summer wakes and starts wailing.

"Can you see to her, Lil?" asks Gran. "She might need to use the potty. Watch she doesn't tip it over her head when she's finished."

"Wiwy!"

When I hear my baby sister calling me, it stirs a memory.

I remember hiding in the hall cupboard in the old house. I remember being petrified to hear a disembodied voice calling my name.

I stand by the kitchen table, almost in a trance. After my near-drowning I pushed all that to the back of my mind. I had almost forgotten that my sister had contacted me somehow – telepathically – and saved my life. Since Millport, I've been so relieved to be alive I haven't tried to see if we could do it again.

Maybe I should try it now. Maybe it could be useful instead of traumatising?

I close my eyes, focus on sending Summer a message.

"Stop crying. I'm on my way."

Summer's wails get louder.

"Lily?" snaps Gran. "What on earth are you doing, standing there with your eyes shut? Go and get Summer!"

I shake myself out of my trance and go and fetch my wee sister. I'll try again some other time.

Chapter 2

Reasons to hate hockey:

- Getting smacked on the ankle by the stick really hurts.
- Ditto getting smacked on the ankle by the ball.
- Hockey is never, ever played on lovely sunny days. Always in the rain.

As the first few weeks passed it began to dawn on me that a lot of my worries about school were a waste of worry time. Aisha has settled into our little group, I've joined a choir and a book club, and nobody has had their head flushed down a toilet. People are even starting to forget I'm famous for nearly dying. And so far, despite my being Jenna's younger sister, the teachers seem to have no opinion on me either way – except for Miss Swanage, the whistle-loving gym teacher. She thinks I'm a lying little toad.

I'm entirely to blame for that, because I'm an expert at staying out of harm's way (well, apart from the drowning incident), and I strongly believe that competitive sport is harmful. So after our first miserable P.E. lesson I prepared a selection of carefully forged notes and started to use them. I'm not stupid; I know I can't avoid P.E every time, so I space out the notes. Plus, I've matured since primary school and think I've developed some excellent skills in writing believable excuses:

To whom it may concern,

Please excuse Lily from P.E. She has been violently sick during the night. I am afraid that if she exerts herself in the gym she may vomit all over the place.

Yours faithfully,
Claire McLean

In week two I used this first note to avoid netball, and then used the same note again two days later when a probationer, Miss Topps, was covering the class. Miss Topps is very energetic and enthusiastic. She announced that we were all going to do an hour of Zumba and it'd be 'fantastic fun'. Then she started demonstrating some fancy dance moves and I decided it probably wouldn't be fantastic fun at all.

The note worked like a charm. Miss Topps became very anxious to get rid of me. She directed me to a bench and allowed me to read while my classmates pranced around to the Zumba music. Score.

Rowan and Georgia choreographed an energetic routine that thrilled Miss Topps to bits. Aisha kept sidling up to me and making me laugh by imitating Miss Topps's comments.

"Ooh, Lily. You're holding that book with *real* energy! Big well done!"

David ended up beside me, in disgrace, after one of his flailing arm moves hit Georgia's shoulder.

Miss Topps thought that nobody could possibly be that unco-ordinated and he must have done it on purpose. The case for the prosecution wasn't helped by Georgia, who clutched her shoulder and wailed. She didn't actually cry – it would have made her mascara run.

"That didn't go well, did it?" sighed David, plonking himself down on the bench. "My career in Zoombering, or whatever it's called, is over before it's begun *and* I've been falsely accused of crimes of violence."

"It could be worse," I said. "At least the rest of the class can carry on now in relative safety. You move like a bear demented by bees."

But the following Tuesday, when I handed Miss Swanage my second note, her frown lines deepened and she gave me a long, hard look with her laser eyes. She read the note aloud, an unmistakably sarcastic note in her voice.

To whom it may concern,

Please excuse Lily from P.E. She was up very late last night, helping to care for her sick grandmother, and although she has managed to drag herself bravely to school, she is completely mentally and physically exhausted.

Yours faithfully,
Claire McLean

"Hmm. Mentally *and* physically exhausted, eh?" Very slowly and deliberately, she placed the note in the pocket of her navy fleece. "Evidence gathering."

But she still let me sit on the bench and read while the rest of the class did mind-numbingly pointless circuits of the playing fields. I almost asked if I could go and sit in the warmth of the library instead, but figured I might be pushing my luck.

Today, in an attempt to avoid the horror of outdoor hockey, I produce my third note. It turns out to be a bad mistake. When Mrs Swanage reads it, her eyebrows knit together to form a single hideous, hairy black caterpillar.

I bite my lip nervously. Perhaps this one isn't quite believable enough:

To whom it may concern,

Please excuse Lily from P.E, as she is recovering from a serious bout of malaria. She is well enough to attend school, but the doctor has recommended that she refrain from strenuous exercise for a few weeks.

Yours faithfully,
Claire McLean

"*Malaria*, Lily?" Mrs Swanage's voice drips acid. "Perhaps you should have opted for a slightly less exotic disease? Yellow fever, perhaps? Dysentery?"

She holds the note up in her bony hands and rips it into two pieces. (She can't rip it to shreds, as I'm sure she would prefer, because we're an Eco School and we'll lose our flag if there's litter in the playground.) She stuffs the pieces into her fleece pocket and glares at me.

I start to panic. Maybe forging notes is a serious crime? Perhaps I'm going to be marched in front of the head teacher and expelled from school. Maybe the police or the fraud squad will be called.

"What is it, Lily, that you dislike so much about sport?" Her voice is cold.

"I like walking, swimming and cycling," I say truthfully. "But I'm not very fond of competitive sports, like netball and hockey."

I don't like gymnastics or running either, and I particularly loathe social dance, but I don't want to be rude, not when P.E. is this woman's chosen vocation.

"Why ever not?" asks Miss Swanage, clearly baffled. "What about team spirit, unity, the joy of winning?"

"But I'm no good at sports, so I'm not an asset to the team. There's not so much joy in constantly losing, Miss Swanage, believe me."

That's half the story, but I can't tell her the whole truth, can I? I can't tell her that clean clothes are hard to come by in our house, and that I am terrified of smelling bad if I get hot and sticky in the gym. I can't tell her that all the shouting and yelling on the pitch reminds me of when my step-dad was around and makes me feel tense and anxious inside.

Maybe she understands a little, because her eyebrows relax into their normal shape.

"Well, if you promise not to try this trick again, we will say no more about it," says Miss Swanage. "Although, I must say, Lily," she adds, totally unable to resist the chance to say more about it, "we only become good at sports if we practise. Practice makes perfect."

Wow, Miss Swanage, impressively original idea there, I think, but wisely don't say. I smile at her instead, feeling dizzy with relief. I'm not going to jail for fraud.

But my relief doesn't last more than a millisecond: now I have to play hockey.

The changing rooms reek of pine disinfectant and smelly trainers. I hide behind a coat stand and struggle into my second-hand gym kit, uncomfortably aware that Jenna's old shorts are too tight for me and my greying polo shirt doesn't smell completely fresh.

Georgia, Jade, Danielle and their pals have no worries about getting changed. They are as loud and confident as the seagulls on Largs beach.

"Hey, Georgia!" shrieks Danielle. "Where did you get those shorts? They are so cute!"

"Topshop in Glasgow, last week. They are nice, aren't they?" Georgia does a little twirl. "I hope Miss Swanage doesn't notice I'm wearing them. Fussy old bat can't stand to see anyone not in regulation blue. She should have joined the army instead of being a teacher."

I speak before I have time to consider the consequences.

"Soldiers wear khaki, not blue."

Georgia gives me one of her puzzled looks: the one that expresses surprise that a lower life form like me has developed the ability to speak.

"I wasn't talking to you, was I?" she snaps. "Are you missing the attention you got at the start of the year, or something? Falling off a pier was a pretty dumb thing to do, by the way."

In the changing room mirror I see my face flush a fiery red. I duck past them and head over to where Rowan and Aisha are tugging on their polo tops.

"This is going to be torture," I mutter.

"Agreed," says Aisha. "I think hockey sticks should be banned. They're dangerous weapons."

"Let's just ban P.E. We could start a petition."

"Oh come on, Lil. It's not so bad," says Rowan, a bit impatiently. Rowan thinks hockey is great. She even agreed with Miss Topps that the stupid Zumba lesson *was* 'fantastic fun'.

I guess friends can't agree about everything, and sport is where our opinions are poles apart. I'm up north with the polar bears and she's down south with the penguins.

Or maybe I'll be down south with the penguins. Penguins don't eat people.

Miss Swanage breaks my train of thought by bustling in and blowing her whistle loudly. (Have I mentioned the whistle is really, really annoying?)

"It's not as if we're sheepdogs," I whisper to Rowan and Aisha. "We can understand verbal instructions. Whistling at us is a violation of our human rights."

Aisha laughs as the room falls silent.

Miss Swanage glances over at us. Perhaps my whisper wasn't quite as whispery as it should have been. Perhaps Mum's right and I'm getting a bit lippy like Jenna.

"Great to see you looking so healthy, Lily!" Miss Swanage yells. She clearly isn't aware that sarcasm is the lowest form of wit. She blasts her whistle again, for no reason. "Right girls, grab your sticks and get outside!"

"Can't wait, Miss Swanage!" I wave my hockey stick in the air.

Sometimes sarcasm is the only way to go.

Today the boys are indoors for basketball, but we have to troop outside into the drizzle. The whole world is leached of colour. Grey clouds scurry across the sky, whipped by an east wind. Rain nips my bare legs.

And yet Georgia is leaping up and down in front of Miss Swanage like an over-enthusiastic Labrador. She is desperate to be team captain. Miss Swanage ignores her and picks Rowan and Molly Baxter.

I relax just a little. At least I have one less nightmare to worry about: Rowan will pick me for her team right away.

But immediately, Rowan's finger points in the wrong direction. She picks Georgia first. And Georgia picks Jade. And Jade picks Danielle. And so on. And so on, until Amy picks Aisha for Molly Baxter's team, which leaves only me and Cassie, who is in a permanent daydream and hasn't even noticed that she is last to be picked.

No, she's not last. I am. Big Cheryl picks Cassie to complete Rowan's team.

"I pick Lily!" calls Aisha, with more enthusiasm than this humiliating situation warrants.

I slink over to join Molly Baxter's team.

"You need to at least *try* this time, Lily." Molly is clearly not thrilled to have me on board. "Being in 'right-back' position doesn't mean you stay *right at the back* and ignore the ball. Play, will you, please?"

"Aye aye, captain," I say, determined to put on a cheerful face even though a little piece of me died when Rowan picked Georgia.

The wind slices through the thin fabric of my polo shirt as we run out onto the pitch and all I want to do is hide.

Ten minutes in, the skin on my legs turns mottled purple and I am drenched. Plus, I have been clobbered three times on the shins by Big Cheryl's hockey stick. Her determination to win is enormous, despite her medium size.

Miraculously though, Miss Swanage gives a piercing blast on her whistle five minutes early. We all leave our positions and run over, slipping and sliding on the Astroturf. I don't think I've ever been so wet and miserable. (Well, ok, apart from the near-drowning thing.)

Miss Swanage waves her arms like windmills. "Come on, girls! Get a move on! This rain isn't going to let up and the playing field is turning into a swamp. Health and safety."

"If she really followed health and safety rules," murmurs Aisha, "she wouldn't have let us risk pneumonia in the first place."

Back in the changing rooms, I dress in a shivery, grumpy huddle, determined not to speak to Rowan. As far as I'm concerned, she broke the friendship code when she failed to pick me for her team.

Problem is, she's equally determined that she is going to speak to me. She stands right in front of me, so that I can't leave unless I push her out of the way. And she knows that pushing people isn't something I do.

"Lily, don't sulk," she says bluntly. "I didn't choose you

for my team because I like to be on the winning side and you really don't care. You don't even bother to hit the ball when it comes near you. You just give it a dirty look, as if it's interrupting your train of thought." She looks at me, smiling, but a little anxious, unsure of how I will react.

I'm unsure too. I pull my sweatshirt over my head, giving myself time to think about it. Part of me still feels betrayed, but there's no doubt that she's right. I don't care about winning, and that could be pretty annoying, I guess, for a person who does.

"Ok." My voice is muffled by the fleecy fabric of my sweatshirt. "Fair enough."

"Next time, if you get picked as team captain, you don't have to choose me."

Oh, big deal, Rowan, I think, still inside my sweatshirt. Two reasons:

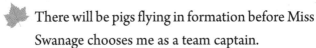 There will be pigs flying in formation before Miss Swanage chooses me as a team captain.

Rowan will never know what it feels like to be picked last. She's popular. I'm so not.

"I've been meaning to ask you something, Lil," Rowan continues, "but I'll wait until I can actually see your face."

I tug my sweatshirt down. "What? Ask me what?"

An electronic buzzer sounds, signalling the end of a period.

"We'd better run," says Rowan, grabbing her bag and blazer and hurrying out the changing room. Aisha and I rush after her through the maze: across the car park, in the main door, up the stairs and along the corridor. All the time I'm thinking…

Ask me what?

Chapter 3

Reasons I like making lists:

- I don't want my brain getting over-stuffed with facts, so I write all the interesting ones down and forget all the boring ones.
- Lists make me feel organised, even when my life's in a messy tangle.
- When I'm feeling anxious, writing a list calms me down. Except that's not going to work today.

Rowan hurries over to the long rows of grey metal lockers, hair still wet from our miserable hockey class. I follow, anxious not to get left behind, and anxious to ask her what she wanted to tell me.

One night during the holidays I had a really bad dream

about getting lost at high school. I was wandering through long, empty corridors, confused and terrified. Suddenly, I fell into a deep black hole and was splashing about in freezing dark water, screaming for help. There were zombies too, in the dream, but there aren't any zombies at high school, at least not until the apocalypse.

Back then I didn't know there were much more terrifying things than zombies at high school: secrets. I've got a horrible feeling Rowan is keeping stuff from me, that she's telling her secrets to Georgia, Jade and Danielle instead.

When I reach my locker, I flick the combination, enjoying the satisfying click it makes when it opens at my command. I love having my own locker with its own secret code. Plus, my bag weighs a ton and if I had to carry all my stuff around I might fall over backwards and someone could post a video of it on YouTube that goes viral, like the sneezing panda.

As I push my gym kit inside, I see a tightly folded piece of paper, light blue, resting in front of a crumpled carrier bag and an old umbrella I've never bothered to throw away. My name's scrawled across the front of the paper. Perhaps it's a note from Rowan – an apology for not picking me for her hockey team or something, though it would be a bit weird if she'd managed to slip it into my locker that quickly without me noticing.

I pull the paper out. Carefully unfold it.

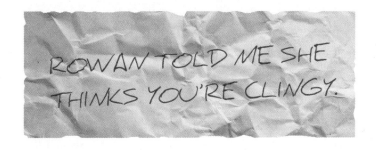

ROWAN TOLD ME SHE
THINKS YOU'RE CLINGY.

That's all it says. It's unsigned.

My stomach clenches. Rowan thinks I'm clingy? I'm so shocked, so horrified, that I crumple the note into a tiny ball. I run towards the nearest bin and throw the note inside, terrified someone might read it, desperate to pretend to myself that it never existed. Because if it's true…

"Lily, come on! We're going to be late!" shouts Aisha.

"Yep," I croak, trying to stop my voice from trembling. Baby koalas are clingy. So are baby marmosets. So is cling film. Not me. I'm not a clingy person. Am I?

I run to catch up with Rowan and Aisha, but I'm overtaken by Georgia and Jade .

"Hi Rowan! Did you get my invite?" calls Jade.

"Yes, thanks. I'd love to come!" says Rowan. "Happy twelfth birthday, by the way!"

"It'll be amazing," crows Georgia. "Jade's mum's friend is a beautician and she's going to do our nails. It'll be like a mini spa-day!"

Aisha nudges me. "Our invitations must have got lost in the post."

I gulp back tears. Not that I would usually care about Jade's silly party – it just makes the note seem more believable. My mind's racing and I feel sick. Is Rowan only pretending to like me? Why would she say a horrible thing like that behind my back? I trail into the English classroom and drop my bag on the floor, never more relieved to see David's cheery grin as I take my seat next to him.

"Spiffing P.E. lesson, was it? I know how much you enjoy a jolly game of hockey." He chortles to himself.

"Lily feels the same about hockey as me," says Aisha. "It sucks all the joy out of life. You're so lucky to get to do basketball this term instead. When's it our turn?"

"I'd enjoy basketball more if I was less Oompa-Loompa sized," sighs David. "The basket is so far out of my reach, they might as well stick it on the moon."

I'm suddenly grateful David and I sat together in English on the first day of school, because it would be mega-awkward to be sitting next to Rowan right now. Of course Aisha is oblivious to all this, and carries on joking as usual. She's had two detentions already from chatting too much in class, and even Rowan's had a detention as a result of sitting next to her. Rowan is still seething about the injustice of that: she likes things to be fair.

If she likes things to be fair, she wouldn't talk behind my back. Would she?

Maybe she would. Things are changing. Rowan has new friends, and I'm not included.

"You look like a drowned rat, by the way," David adds, equally oblivious to my worries.

"That's an incredibly tactless remark, Dave, considering I nearly drowned right in front of you not two months ago," I retort, but I am almost tearfully glad that David is his normal, jokey self. At least I've still got him and Aisha, even if I lose Rowan.

Unabashed, David peers at me through his wire-rimmed glasses. "You looked worse then, I guess, but not much. You're actually dripping on your desk."

He's right. My hair is soaking wet. I'm going to get double pneumonia and Miss Swanage still won't believe I'm too ill to do P.E. Until I drop dead on the hockey pitch. She'll have to believe me then.

And if I got ill and died, would Rowan even care? Would she miss me or would she just be glad I'd stopped clinging?

"Here. Use this." David reaches into his bag and passes me a small, folded hand towel. "I don't even have gym today. My mum clearly stole the 'Be prepared' motto from the Scouts and added 'Always carry a clean towel, just in case.' Though I guess if the zombie apocalypse happens, a towel will be handy for wiping up the blood."

I rub at my wet hair and shake my head at the same time.

"Steel shutters and an electrified fence would be handier." I try to join in, because David loves a bit of zombie chat.

"True. Then you could avoid the blood in the first place because they wouldn't be able to get in your house and eat your brains. Good thinking."

"Of course, you'll need supplies of tinned food and—"

I stop mid-sentence. Mr Barton is looming over my desk. I can't believe I'm about to be told off by a teacher for the second time in one morning.

"Lily, I'm sorry to trouble you, but could you abandon your discussion on how to survive an invasion by legions of the undead, and instead focus on our current predicament: we have insufficient copies of *War Horse* and you'll have to share."

He grins at me and hands me a bedraggled copy. Mr Barton is definitely my favourite teacher, ever.

The lesson begins. I love this book, but parts of it are so sad they make me want to cry. While Mr Barton is reading aloud, my mind wanders helplessly back to Rowan's comment in the changing room, and to the horrible note in my locker.

I've been meaning to ask you something...

...Rowan told me she thinks you're clingy.

What's going on?

Was she trying to hint at this by picking Georgia for the hockey team? Does she think we've outgrown our friendship? Have I lost Rowan forever?

At lunchtime Aisha and I go to our School of Rock choir. Usually I enjoy singing but today my voice feels choked and croaky. In the afternoon Rowan and I are in different groups in science class, but together again in maths at the end of the day. We don't get a chance to chat though, because Mrs Wightman is old and strict and doesn't approve of pupils talking in class. As far as Mrs Wightman is concerned, active learning is new-fangled nonsense. She rattles off instructions, machine-gun fast, and we sit in rows, heads down, like children in a Victorian school.

By the time the home bell rings, I'm shattered. Aisha has to rush off to catch the ferry and Rowan goes straight to after-school gymnastics club. I walk home with David as usual, my worries weighing me down like wet clothes on a drowning person.

"You alright, Lil?" asks David. "You're not engaging with my witty banter."

"I'm fine," I lie. "Just tired. I'll be glad to get home to chill."

But when I arrive home, I find Mum has other plans. She's home from work early and is peering into the oven, an apron around her waist, her hair brushed and glossy, like a pretend mum in a TV advert. Jenna comes in behind me and we both gawp, open-mouthed. Who is this alien?

"Hi girls. I've invited Brian to dinner," Mum says airily. "I thought it would be lovely if you all met."

Brian is Mum's new boyfriend. She met him when she served him a latte and doughnut in the café on Largs promenade. He told her about his obsession with trains, and for some bizarre reason she didn't back away, muttering excuses. Although I don't suppose it is that bizarre, given her track record for choosing unsuitable men. Her last partner, my step-dad and the father of Bronx, Hudson and Summer, was an alcoholic, aggressive and scary when drunk. To be fair to Brian, he doesn't sound anything like that, just very geeky. Apparently, apart from trains, his other interest is ornithology, which actually gives him and me something in common, though I'm not admitting that to anyone.

When Brian arrives, the boys are watching TV. Summer's plonked in-between them, playing with Roary, the toy lion I gave her. Jenna and I are hovering, expecting the worst. Mum is crashing around in the kitchen.

"I can't believe she has invited The Trainspotter tonight," hisses Jenna. "I wanted an early night. I'm shattered."

She does look tired, and there are dark shadows under her eyes, which might just be smeared eyeliner.

The doorbell rings and Mum rushes to answer it. We hear her voice, weirdly high-pitched, and another, deep and growly.

"This is Brian, kids!" she declares, dragging a tall, bearded man into the living room.

"Wiwy! Wiwd Fing!" Summer doesn't like strangers. She leaps from the couch, clings to me and wails in terror. Not a great start.

"It's alright, Summer. It's not one of the monsters from *Where the Wild Things Are*, honestly, it isn't," I say soothingly. "It's only Mum's friend, Brian."

"Hi, kids. Nice to meet you all." Brian strokes his beard nervously and hands Mum a bunch of wilting chrysanthemums. "These are for you, babe."

Jenna and I gaze at him in silent horror. *Babe????*

"Ha, ha!" chuckles Hudson from the couch. "Brian called Mum a pig. Babe's a pig, isn't she, Lil?"

"I don't think that's what he meant, Hudson," I say. "But yes, Babe is a piglet in a story."

Brian looks mortified.

"A very cute one," I add hastily, while Mum fusses over the flowers.

"Ooh, these are beautiful," she trills. "Jenna, could you put Brian's lovely flowers in water, please?"

Jenna rolls her eyes rudely. "Sure, I'll try and save them. Are these the ones they sell on the garage forecourt for £2.99, Brian? I think you've been ripped off."

"Jenna! That's enough!" snaps Mum. "Bronx and Hudson, turn off the TV and move up the couch so Brian can sit down."

The television blares. The boys start to squabble over which channel they're going to watch when *Scooby Doo* finishes.

I screw up my eyes and try to send Bronx a telepathic message like Summer did to me: *Switch off the television and be polite.*

"I'm having the remote now! I want to watch *Ben 10!*" squeals Hudson.

"You're a big ugly moron! It's my turn!" shrieks Bronx.

Nope, still not telepathic.

"Boys, where are your manners?" Mum barks.

Bronx looks a bit blank, as he has no idea where his

manners are, and then horrified, as Mum switches off the television.

"Mum!!! That's not fair! *Ben 10* is coming on!"

Mum's eyes glitter and her mouth becomes a thin, hard line. "Brian has come for dinner, Bronx. Say hello nicely, please."

Bronx looks Brian up and down and then announces in a very loud voice: "Lily, that man's got long hair AND a bald head. The top of his head's all shiny."

Brian looks appalled, as if he had been totally unaware of his baldness up to this point. Mum tries to laugh it off, but her laugh sounds tinkly and nervous.

"Bronx, it's very rude to make personal remarks. Say sorry," I insist.

"Hello Brian. Sorry Brian," says Bronx. "Brian, why does your hair grow out the sides of your head and not out the top?"

Things pick up slightly at dinner. The boys sit quietly, staring at Brian. I pick at my food, worries about Rowan whirling round in my head. Then Bronx elbows Hudson, who knocks over his plastic cup. Sprite splashes all over Brian's beige trousers.

"Look, Mum!" shrieks Bronx. "It looks like Brian's peed himself! His trousers are all wet!"

"Never mind, it was a little accident!" says Brian, his smile not quite reaching his eyes.

"It was a *wee* accident, you mean! You *weed* yourself!" howls Bronx, loving his own joke.

Bronx and Hudson might behave like wild animals but at least they've got the excuse of being only five and six. Jenna makes her feelings about Brian crystal clear and yawns widely while he talks to her about trains. He tries me instead.

"Lily, your mother tells me that you are interested in the natural world. I read today that Scotland's population of corncrakes increased by forty-five per cent last year. Isn't that amazing?"

It is pretty amazing, actually, but Jenna glares at me, and I know better than to side with the enemy.

"Hmm, I guess," I mumble.

Brian gives up and goes back to the tricky task of swallowing Mum's disgustingly stringy pork casserole and lumpy mashed potato.

"I just *love* birds." Mum tries to fill the awkward silence.

That's a total fib, unless you count roast turkey at Christmas or chicken kievs, I think.

Brian smiles at Mum and studiously ignores our rude behaviour right until dessert when Hudson starts a fight with Bronx while Mum is out of the room. They roll around under the table, shrieking abuse.

"You're a big poo! I hate you!" yells Bronx. He aims a kick at Hudson, who kicks back.

Unfortunately Hudson doesn't have very good gross motor skills and the kick connects with Brian's shin. Brian lets out a yelp of pain, which startles Summer, who is overtired and really should be in bed by now. She squeals like a braking express train. Then Jenna starts to laugh and Brian announces that he has to get home because he's had a long day.

He doesn't even finish his Morrison's apple pie and tinned custard.

Mum's furious with us and we get sent straight to bed. I'm sorry her evening hasn't gone as planned, but relieved that I can skip the boys' story. All I want is to go to bed and think about what happened at school today.

Chapter 4

Reasons Jenna and I don't fight quite so much any more:

- She got a fright when I nearly died, although the effects are beginning to wear off.
- There's more space in the new house.
  We have a common enemy: Boring Brian, the baldy beardy geek.
- She's too busy sleeping all the time to fight with me.

"Did you see the *The Phantom Menace* on TV last night?" David asks at break next morning. "It looks a bit dated nowadays, compared to the new movies."

"Nope," says Aisha. "I've got a life."

"What, on Millport?" David laughs. "Really?"

"Ha, ha. You're hilarious. Millport is buzzing, I'll have you know. Isn't it, Lil?"

They stand there, grinning, waiting for me to join in. Rowan's smiling at me too. Rowan, who's going around school telling people she thinks I'm clingy.

"Millport's great," I say. "*The Phantom Menace*, not so much."

"What were you up to last night, Lil?" asks Rowan.

"Nothing."

She doesn't push, but she looks worried, as if she knows I'm keeping secrets too.

Once again I won't get another chance to speak properly to Rowan because Mum asked me to nip back home at lunchtime to make sure Jenna gets to her doctor's appointment.

I know it's not Mum's fault that she has to work, but it's a long walk, and I grudge every step. Everybody else will be buying hot soup or a ham sandwich in the school canteen. Some of the fifth and sixth years might head for the takeaway down the road for chips and curry sauce. I will hardly have time to grab some toast before its time to hurry back to school.

When I reach our road, my footsteps slow. It's a long terrace of local authority houses, all with tidy little front gardens. Well, almost all. Our house has an actual jungle, front and back. I tell the boys it's a wildlife garden and more environmentally friendly than the ones with plastic furniture and concrete patios. And sometimes, when the sun is shining and butterflies are flittering among the buttercups, it does look almost pretty. But today it just seems ugly, untidy and neglected. A rusting bike lies abandoned among the nettles.

The garden looks the way I feel: tired, soaked and unwanted.

I just want to get home, eat some toast and wallow in self-pity about Rowan, but our neighbour Mr Henderson is trimming the hedge around his tiny but immaculate lawn as I approach the house. Maybe his wrinkly old skin protects him from the elements. He waves his hedge clippers at me accusingly.

"You're home from school early today. Don't tell me it's another holiday? You've just had the whole summer off!"

"It'll be the September weekend soon," I say. "But I'm just home for lunch today."

"Wasn't like that in my day," he grumbles. "We didn't get all those holidays from school. And we got the belt when we misbehaved. Never did us any harm. Bring back the belt, I say."

"I'll suggest it at the next Pupil Council Meeting, Mr Henderson," I say, though I'm thinking that maybe if Mr

Henderson hadn't been belted as a wee boy, he wouldn't have turned into such a grouchy old man.

I don't know why Mr Henderson thinks it's always the holidays. The summer holidays felt short to me this year, and not just because I spent half of it being haunted by my baby sister and some of it in hospital. We were mega-busy moving house after that. Well, some of us were busy. Some of us just kept on fighting over the television remote.

First, we had to clear the old house and throw out lots of broken furniture and toys, which wasn't as straightforward as it sounds. Every time I attempted to bin one of their hundreds of broken action figures, there were yelps of dismay from Bronx or Hudson.

"But Lil, that's my favouritist guy! You can't throw him out! His eyes light up!"

"Um, no they don't, not any more. And somebody has amputated his left leg."

"But he's still my favouritist ever! I need to keep him!"

If they carry on like that, Bronx and Hudson will end up on one of those television programmes about hoarders who can't get into their own houses because of all the junk they've collected over the years.

The next job was cleaning the new house, because an old man had lived in it before, and possibly died in it, and it smelled weird. The cleaning took ages, and Gran barked orders like a grumpy sergeant major until Jenna was ready to explode.

"I'm not her skivvy!" she shrieked one morning, wisely waiting until Gran had gone outside to nark at the bin men. "If she doesn't stop bossing me about, I'm going to tip this bucket of soapy water over her head!"

Decorating was a lot more fun. With some not very useful help from Bronx and Hudson, Jenna and I worked really hard to paint over the previous tenant's hideous turquoise-and-magenta colour scheme.

"The old guy must have been colour blind," Mum gasped when she saw the walls. (Which was the pot calling the kettle black, since she was wearing Oxfam's finest lilac floral skirt, orange beret and lime mohair poncho).

Thanks to Gran, all the rooms are now a dull-but-inoffensive magnolia. She bought several rollers and vats of paint with her B&Q old-person's discount card. Sadly, Mum's clothes are as offensive as ever.

The best part of moving was how well Jenna and I got on during that time. We have been getting on a lot better since my near-drowning in the summer, though she isn't being nearly as nice to me now as she was in the week after I got out of hospital. That week was amazing – she even moved out of her room so I could recuperate in peace. It was a massive sacrifice, as it meant she had to spend a week sharing a room with the gruesome twosome. I think she came close to committing fratricide that week.

Anyway, we still fight, but since she nearly lost me, Jenna doesn't scream at me to get lost so often. The fact that we have more space to avoid each other now helps. Compared to our last house, this one is a palace. There's no hall cupboard for a den, but I don't need one: not when I've got my own room. Jenna guards her new bedroom fiercely against potential invasion by siblings, but I don't know why she thinks we would want to go in there. It's as dark, smelly and sinister as an animal's lair; the sort of animal that objects strongly to being disturbed, like a grizzly bear or a rattlesnake.

Yup, I no longer have to share a room with my two younger brothers, a fact which still makes me feel happy every time I think it, happy enough to want to do cartwheels across the grass (if cartwheels were my thing, which they're not). It's a tiny little room, but its mine and I love it.

Gran bought me a new sky-blue duvet set and a fluffy cream rug, which I am trying very hard to keep nice. Bronx and Hudson are banned, but Summer is allowed in, unless I'm writing in my red leather notebook, or reading, or texting Rowan on my new mobile – not that I'll be texting her much from now on. Mum got me the mobile for my birthday, 'to stay safe'. I guess she thinks that next time I fall into the sea I'll be able to take my phone out of my pocket, give her a call, tell her I'm drowning and she'll be able to rush to the rescue.

"Jen!" I call, throwing my bag on my sky-blue bed.

Silence.

I trudge reluctantly along the corridor and knock on Jenna's door.

"Jen! Please tell me you're awake! It's half past twelve!"

No reply.

Losing patience, I yank at the handle and shove the door open. The floor is strewn with clothes and dirty plates. The curtains are closed and the room smells stale.

"Jenna, it stinks in here! How can you even breathe?"

Again, no reply.

I stride over and tug angrily at the curtains, then fling the window wide open so that the wind whirls in. The striped curtains flap like flags. Then I stand over the bed and drag her duvet onto the floor.

Finally, I get a reaction.

"What the heck are you doing!" Jenna shrieks. "Get lost, Lily! Leave me alone, for goodness' sake!"

"Stop shouting," I snap back. "Don't take your bad temper out on me, Jenna McLean. Mum asked me to get you out of your bed in time, so I am only following orders.

If you want to argue about it, speak to Gran. She'll be home first."

I am reasonably confident that Jenna won't speak to Gran. Not many people argue with her. She's a big, scary woman, and arguing is her area of expertise.

"Get me up in time for what?" Jenna looking genuinely baffled.

"The doctor's appointment. Remember? She thinks you're ill. Doesn't realise you're just skiving."

Jenna groans. She grabs the duvet from the floor and wraps it tightly round her body.

I reach out and shake her, gently. "Come on Jen. Be fair. I need to head back to school in ten minutes. Do you want some cheese on toast?"

There's a muffled sound from under the duvet, which I guess is a yes, so I leave the room and head down to the kitchen. It's bigger than our old one, and has an actual table and chairs where we can, in theory, eat civilised family meals. In practice, we do no such thing, except on Gran days, or Brian days, apparently.

I haven't checked the fridge, so I'm not sure if I can deliver on my promise of cheese on toast, but luckily Gran was here yesterday, so the kitchen isn't empty – like Georgia's brain.

I didn't mean that about Georgia. She isn't stupid – not

at all. But I know she doesn't like me, which makes it so much worse that Rowan picked her instead of me for the hockey team. I've been thinking about it since yesterday and I've figured it's probably Georgia who put that note in my locker. It's the sort of mean thing she'd do.

"You look totally spaced, Lil. Why are you standing in the middle of the kitchen holding two slices of bread?" asks Jenna, who is magically out of her bed, dressed and ready to go out – all in the time it has taken me to open a packet of cheddar, cut a few slices and turn on the grill. "You'll need another slice if you're planning to juggle. Or if you're making toast, the grill is over there, roughly in the same place as the oven."

"I am totally aware of the grill's whereabouts, thanks." I look at her crumpled top. "The ironing board is in the cupboard to the left of the fridge, if you're ever looking for it."

"Ironing is for numpties. I've got better things to do with my life."

"Yeah, like lie in your smelly pit 'til lunchtime. You could've been tidying up round here. Helping Mum."

Jenna lifts the kettle over to the sink and turns the tap on, hard.

"Give it a rest, Lil. If Mum spent more time at home and less time with Boring Brian, the trainspotting geek, the house would be immaculate."

I rush to Mum's defence. "They've only been going out a little while. She doesn't spend *that* much time with him."

"Nobody could, without dying of terminal boredom," sneers Jenna. "He's the most boring man on the planet. Gran's magnolia paint is more exciting."

She launches into an imitation of Brian's monotonous voice from last night.

"'Did you know, girls, that the Largs train line effectively becomes *two single tracks* after Saltcoats?'"

I giggle, even though I know she's being a bit mean. It was not a successful dinner and Mum was still fizzing mad this morning, but I'm going to make the most of being on Jenna's team while I can.

In a few minutes the cheese is bubbling under the grill and Jenna has made two cups of tea. The smell of toast improves everything – even Jenna's mood. I place the food on the table and we sit together, crunching on the slightly burnt toast and slurping strong tea.

"What will you say when the doctor asks you what's wrong?" I ask.

"I don't know," says Jenna. "Feeling faint, dizzy... tired, I guess."

"What about 'I can't be bothered to go to school so I tell my mum I'm not well'?" I say, a bit sharply. I reckon Jenna's excuses are just a magnified version of my P.E. sick notes.

She doesn't snap back, but puts down her cup and looks at me rather sadly. I notice suddenly her pale, chalky skin and the dark shadows like purple bruises under her eyes.

I feel panicked, thinking maybe I have completely failed to notice that my own sister is dying.

"Jenna?" I say. "Are you really not well? Seriously not well?"

She shrugs. "I just don't feel great, Lil. Stop looking at me like that. I haven't got cancer or anything. Gran thinks I might be anaemic. She says the doc will give me iron tablets and I'll be fixed."

"Are you sure that's what's wrong? Gran isn't the big expert on illness she pretends to be, you know. She told Mum that Summer had measles and it turned out she was just allergic to our washing powder."

Jenna shivers at the memory. "That cheap stuff brought me out in a rash too. Anyway, that's why I'm going to the doctor, to get a proper diagnosis. Honestly, Lil. Will you stop looking so mournful! You are such a worrier."

"I like to think the worst and then whatever happens is never quite as bad." I smile feebly.

"Well, it's giving me the creeps. You're looking at me as if I'm a ghostly vision. Stop it. Finish your toast and get back to school. Did you know that Mr Diarmid stands behind the gatepost, waiting to pounce on anyone who tries to sneak in late?"

I know she is deliberately giving me something else to worry about, but I fall for it anyway. I sprint upstairs, grab my bag and run out the door. "Bye, Jen. Good luck at the doctor's."

"Bye Lil. Thanks for waking me. Gran would have killed me if I'd missed my appointment."

My sister just thanked me. This is a momentous day. It almost makes me forget I might be losing my best friend. I pull out my phone as I hurry back to school in the rain, just in case Rowan has texted. But there's nothing. Well, there's a text from David saying

> C u l8r

but I'm pretty sure that counts as nothing. Of course I'll see him later. I see him nearly every day of my life. He's my best friend, after Rowan.

Maybe I should text her, or just confront her about the note and find out what it is she has been meaning to ask me. But I am afraid to learn the answer. As my gran, the queen of cliché, would say: 'what you don't know can't hurt you' and 'ignorance is bliss'.

My stomach lurches when Aisha and I bump into Rowan in the corridor on her way to I.C.T.

I can't think of anything casual to say, so I jump straight to it: "Er Rowan, what was that thing you were going to ask me yesterday?"

"Oh, nothing! Doesn't matter now." She smiles, and sounds so normal, as if nothing has changed between us.

What does she mean? Why doesn't it matter now? Is it too late?

I'm so preoccupied I forget I won't see Rowan in the afternoon, as she isn't in my I.C.T. class and afterwards it's no-talking-allowed maths with Mrs Wightman again. Then Rowan has after-school netball, with Georgia of course, while David and I are going to book club. I can stay blissfully ignorant after all. Though I feel more anxious than blissful, to be honest: I worry about what Rowan wanted to ask me; and I'm stressed about Jenna and her doctor's appointment.

I send Jenna a text, but she doesn't reply.

I can feel my heart beginning to thump hard in my chest as I grab the broken umbrella out of my locker at the end of the day. What if Jenna is really ill? What if the doctor has sent her straight to hospital?

And then my stomach flips again.

Another neatly folded note tumbles out from beneath the umbrella.

I don't know whether it's a new note or if I missed seeing it yesterday. It was so well hidden it could have been there for ages. But it's definitely meant for me: my name's scrawled across the front in big capital letters, just like the first note.

I don't read it. I can't face it; just push it into my schoolbag.

Chapter 5

Stuff that scares me:

- Zombie movies. David loves them, but they give me the creeps.
- Fierce dogs. Every dog should be like Finn, Rowan's big daft Labrador.
- Losing my best friend.

When I get home after book club I can hear Gran crashing pans in the sink, which can only mean that she's in a very bad mood. She's complaining loudly too, either to herself or to Summer.

"Wee fiends! Fighting again! I don't have a moment's peace in my old age. Potty training, running about after all these weans, pushing buggies! What happened to spending my twilight years dozing in a chair in front of the telly, eh?"

"Hi, Gran!" I call. "See you in a minute!"

First I run upstairs to check if Jenna's hiding in her room to avoid Gran, which would be entirely understandable. But Jenna's room is empty, clothes scattered, duvet still lying on the floor in a crumpled heap. My mind races. Surely she wouldn't have gone out with her friends when she's been feeling so ill? Gran would never let her do that after she's been off school.

I put the duvet back neatly on the bed and head downstairs. Before I can worry too much about Jenna I've got to take care of the terrible twosome. The boys are squabbling loudly in the living room, bawling above the frenetic whoops of the CBBC presenter. Why do children's presenters always have to screech like frenzied parrots? I guess I'm not their target audience, it's kids like Bronx and Hudson. And shouting is their thing.

"Bronx, give that back, you big smelly poop!"

"It's mine! I had it first!"

They are yelling at each other so loudly that the neighbours must be able to hear them. No wonder Mr Henderson hates the school holidays. No wonder Gran is in a foul temper.

"I'll tell Gran on you! Awww, you've broken it! You did that on purpose!"

"Owwww! That was sore! Gran! Hudson punched me!"

I stomp into the room, turn off the television and stand in front of it, arms folded. My actions are rewarded by howls of outrage.

"We were watching that, Lil! That's our favouritist programme!"

"You weren't watching, you were fighting. Watching looks like this…" I sit on the couch and stare, glass-eyed, at the television. Then I stand up again and wave the remote like a magic wand. "If you *promise* me you'll watch, not fight, then I will switch the television back on. If you carry on fighting, then I will take the remote and put it in Jenna's room."

That works. The boys look horrified. They know they would never be able to retrieve it without risking life and limb.

"I promise, Lil," says Hudson. "I won't make a single sound and I won't punch Bronx again, even though he broke Michaelangelo, who is my favouritist Turtle."

"It was an accident. I never even touched it. The arm came off in my hand. Honest it did, Lil."

"Whatever, Bronx. I'm sure it can be fixed…" I say, doubtful that it can be fixed. "But what about your promise?"

I receive a solemn promise from Bronx, too, that he will sit quietly for the rest of his life. I click the remote and place it back on the coffee table.

Peace restored, I leave them to their television viewing and head into the kitchen.

Summer is sitting quietly on the floor, unnoticed by Gran, beside an open cupboard. She has upturned an enormous box of Rice Krispies and is happily cramming handfuls of it into her mouth.

"Hi Gran. Hi Summer," I say. "What are you two up to? Have you had a good day, Gran?"

Crash!

Gran throws the grill pan into the sink. Water splashes across the floor and Quipp, our big ginger tom, leaps for cover.

Maybe not, then.

At least Summer is in a good mood. She grins and offers me a fistful of soggy rice cereal.

"Wiwy! Clackle, pop!" says cheerfully, spitting Rice Krispies as she speaks. "Yummy Klispies."

"Um, no thanks, Summer. I'll pass," I say. "Is everything alright, Gran?"

"I'm too old for all this," Gran grumbles, without turning round. She is scrubbing furiously at the blackened grill pan, and I guiltily remember that Jenna and I didn't clean up after ourselves earlier.

Gran finds my three younger siblings hard going. She's

Jenna and my dad's mother; Bronx, Hudson and Summer are my step-dad's children. I wish she would like the wee ones more, but to be perfectly honest, Bronx and Hudson don't make it easy for her. They're a handful, at home and in school.

Hudson has just started in P3 and he's already lost Golden Time for being cheeky. Apparently he told Miss Smart that she has a whiskery chin and she wasn't one bit amused. Mum thought the whole incident was hilarious, but I gave Hudson a huge row. I don't want my old P7 teacher, Mrs McKenzie, hearing that my brothers are monsters.

Gran turns away from the sink and wipes her reddened, wrinkly hands on a tea towel. They tremble as she puts it back on the worktop.

"I need a sit down. My knees are killing me," she says wearily.

I close the kitchen cupboard door before Gran notices the spilled cereal. I'll clear it up later.

"Summa's Klispies!" Summer shouts. "Bling back Summa's Klispies, Wiwy!"

"Here, I think Roary needs a cuddle." I hand over her beloved stuffed lion before she can say any more. I bought Roary for her birthday earlier this year and she adores it.

Summer's face glows with pleasure as she hugs the

tattered toy. "Woawy hungly for Klispies," she insists, and tries to stuff some stray puffs of rice into the lion's sewn-on mouth. Its pink fluorescent mane is looking decidedly stringy and its orange fur is filthy. I'll need to wrestle Roary off Summer and wash it before she gets a disease.

"What's that child saying?" grumbles Gran. "I can't understand a word she says."

"She says she likes being with Granny," I say. "She says you make yummy dinners."

"Yummy dinners?" sighs Gran. "Well, I'm glad the wee soul's happy. But I'm shattered after running about after her all day. I don't think I'm up to cooking dinner tonight, yummy or otherwise."

"Sit down, Gran. I'll put the kettle on." If Jenna is missing, the last thing we need is a tired, crabbit Gran in charge. But I know just how to calm her down: get her talking about the weather. After illness and death, the weather is Gran's favourite conversation topic. "I'll take the boys out for a walk, Gran. They'll be wild because they've been stuck indoors all day at school. The weather's dreadful, isn't it?"

"Oh, it's a disgrace. The daft lassie on the telly got it completely wrong. If I'd listened to her, I might have hung out a washing, and now where would it be? Half way out to sea, that's where."

"At least we don't get typhoons like they do in Japan,

or tornadoes like they do in America," I say, though to be honest I think Gran would love it if we did.

I don't tell her the real reason I want to go out: that I want to go and look for Jenna. She should have been home long ago, but if I remind Gran about that, she'll immediately assume that something awful – probably fatal – has happened to her. Gran is a bigger worrier than me sometimes.

We look out of the kitchen window. Soggy leaves, stripped from the beech tree by the wind, clog the drains and gutters. Our wheelie bin lies on its side, the lid flapping. Lashing rain bounces off the concrete slabs. Autumn's arrived.

"It's not a day for a walk, Lil," Gran sighs.

"We'll just go for a dash along the prom. The boys will enjoy looking at the big waves. I'll not go near the sea, though. Nowhere near, I promise."

I still feel very guilty about how badly my accident in the summer upset my gran. She talks about it a lot, even, embarrassingly, to complete strangers in the queue at the supermarket.

Suddenly Gran smiles at me and her face creases into a zillion wrinkles. She reaches for her voluminous leather bag and pulls out her purse.

"Take the baby too, Lil. And get some fish and chips for tea. I can't face cooking tonight. My arthritis is playing up something terrible. It must be this cold weather making me so creaky."

"Are you sure, Gran? Fish and chips are expensive. I could run to the shops instead and make us all beans on toast, if you like."

"You're an awfy good lass, Lil. I don't know what we'd all do without you." She holds out a £20 note. "But I won this at the bingo last week, so I can afford a treat."

I take the proffered money and stick it in my jacket pocket. Things are looking up. "Bronx! Hudson! Get your jackets and wellies. We're going out to get a chippy!"

There's a loud roar of delight.

"Can I get sausage?" asks Hudson, who hates fish unless it's finger-shaped.

"Don't let them put vinegar on my chips, Lil. It makes them taste disgusterous," says Bronx, pulling his wellington boots onto the wrong feet.

"You can tell them yourself, Bronx. You're a big boy." I pull his boots back off and help him put them on correctly.

Summer's content in her waterproofed buggy, but the boys' happy grins fade when we walk out of the door into the torrential rain and bitter wind.

"Maybe you could go and get the chips, Lil," suggests Bronx.

"We won't fight," wheedles Hudson. "We won't bother

Gran. We'll sit like statues and watch *Ben 10*, with the sound down even, maybe."

They huddle against the front door, trying to look pitiful. It almost works. The weather is hideous, and for a millisecond I'm sorely tempted to forget the whole plan. But I want to find Jenna. And poor Gran needs a bit of peace and quiet. I don't want her giving up on us. Mum needs her. *We* need her.

"Um, no. If you don't come, you don't get. Gran's allowed to stay in the house because she's an old lady and you've tired her out with all your nonsense. And poor Mum isn't home from work yet, so we need to get hers too; and fried chicken for Jenna, because that's her favourite. Come on now. The quicker we move, the sooner we'll be home."

I shove the buggy purposefully onward, while the boys trail after me. The one on Main Street would be brightly lit and cheery and welcoming, but it's too far to walk on a day like today. We'll go to the one on Greenock Road instead.

"But, Lil!" wails Hudson. "It's all rainy and windy! The rain's nipping my face!"

"Stop moaning, Hud. You won't dissolve. But hold on tight to the buggy, just in case you get blown away."

On Largs promenade the sky and sea merge, a sullen grey. Waves crash angrily against the rocks, spitting froth.

Driving rain smacks against our faces and the wind tugs at our clothes and hair.

"The waves are humungous!" Bronx wheels around like a windblown gull. "It's like a Sue Nammy, isn't it Lily?"

"No, Bronx. It's nothing like a tsunami. But keep back from the wall, will you, please? I don't want you being swept out to sea. The lifeboat men have enough to do without having to come and pull you out of the water."

As I walk, I make a list in my head of my worries: the disastrous forged sick notes, Rowan's mysterious question, Jenna's illness, the note in my locker...

I remember with a sickening lurch, that there's another note inside my bag.

I don't understand what's going on. Nobody knows my locker's four-digit code, so someone must be sliding notes through the vent. And if the second note is anything like the first, it's going to make me feel a whole lot worse.

When we finally reach the chippy, there's a long queue. We are going to have to hang around a while, but at least it's warm and dry inside.

Hudson and Bronx immediately start bickering. It always amazes me how they can start a fight over absolutely nothing.

"I'm wetter than you, Hudson," starts Bronx, triumphantly shaking himself like a dog and spattering the other people in the queue.

An elderly lady tuts and glares at us.

"No way. I'm zillions wetter than you," says Hudson. "Even my *pants* are wet!" He tugs at his trousers.

I shake my head at him, anxious that he doesn't show his underwear to the whole queue. Unfortunately, my hair is dripping wet and the people in the queue get sprayed with water again.

The old lady tuts even louder and wipes at her face with a tissue.

"You are both equally wet. You spent exactly the same amount of time in exactly the same amount of rain. And if you don't stop your nonsense," I lower my voice and narrow my eyes, "we will leave this chip shop right now and you'll get nothing for dinner. I mean it. Nothing."

Wisely, Bronx and Hudson stop squabbling. At last, we reach the counter and I give my order to the girl. "Three fish suppers, one chicken and chips, two kid's sausage—"

"Lily! Lily!" Bronx tugs sharply on my arm.

"I told you, Bronx. You need to tell the girl yourself if you don't want vinegar on your chips."

"But Lil, look," he whines, tugging at my arm again. He

goes to the window and rubs at it with his sleeve to give me a clearer view outside.

"Look, Lil, there's Jenna. She isn't wearing her jacket. That's silly, isn't it, Lil?"

I look out and see my big sister huddled in a shop doorway opposite us. Her clothes are sodden and her dyed-black hair is plastered to her head. She's laughing up at a thin boy smoking a cigarette in a grey hoodie. He looks familiar.

I stare through the drizzle. Where have I seen him before?

And with a sinking heart realise it is Kai Dixon, the ned who Mr Diarmid sent packing on our first day. The one who swore and spat on the pavement. The one who Aisha's brother said was a fighter. And a thief.

Chapter 6

The pros and cons of telling on Jenna:

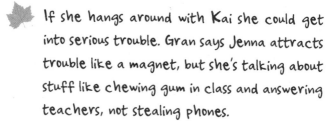

- If she hangs around with Kai she could get into serious trouble. Gran says Jenna attracts trouble like a magnet, but she's talking about stuff like chewing gum in class and answering teachers, not stealing phones.
- If I tell Mum and Gran on her she'll be raging with me. And Jenna's temper is fierce.
- If I tell Mum and Gran she'll never trust me again.

Jenna thinks smoking is vile. She can't stand the smell... says it makes her want to be sick. So what's she doing standing right next to someone who is puffing stinky smoke all over her hair and clothes? Someone who has such a bad reputation that the Depute Head once threatened to call the police on him?

I abandon the boys and Summer in the chip shop and run outside into the rain.

"Jenna!" I yell, waving my arms frantically. "I'm getting chips! Come over! Jenna, we're here!"

But she doesn't hear me, or see me – or if she does, she pretends she hasn't. She leaves the shelter of the doorway and walks off towards the promenade with Kai. He throws his cigarette on the ground and swings an arm round her shoulder. She smiles up at him like one of those pale, soppy heroines in her beloved vampire books.

My first instinct is to run after her and shout that she needs to come home. I could make an excuse, say it's because she doesn't look well… I could tell her I've bought her chicken and chips for dinner. But I need to go back inside, round up the boys, collect our fish suppers and push Summer's buggy through the howling wind and torrential rain all the way home.

My second thought is to rush home and tell Gran and Mum. I know telling will not do anything to improve my relationship with Jenna. It's not that I want to be a telltale. But I need adult backup. I don't think I can fix this one on my own.

The whole way home, I'm looking for answers. Why's

Jenna hanging around with Kai Dixon? What did the doctor say to her? What did Rowan want to ask me? Does she really think I'm clingy? Who's leaving horrible notes in my locker?

"I wish I'd never come on this stupid walk," wails Bronx. "Summer is so lucky!"

He's not wrong. A flash of lightning cuts the grey sky, icy rain blows in our faces and the wind whips our hair into knots. By the time we reach our house, Summer, safe underneath her plastic raincover, is the only one of us who isn't wet, cold and miserable.

"Wow! What possessed you all to go out for a walk on a day like this?" laughs Mum, as she pulls off Hudson's jacket and flings it carelessly over the banister. A puddle forms on the carpet. "You're all soaked to the skin!"

"Mummy!" Summer gleefully drums her fists against the plastic rain cover.

"Hi, Mum!" yells Bronx. "Hudson and me are both wet right through to our pants! Sure we are, Lily?"

I push the buggy into the hall and hold up the carrier bag triumphantly.

"Fish and chips, courtesy of Gran," I say.

"Good old Gran," says Mum. She's smiling and I know she's pleased about the chips, but her tone is slightly sarky.

Mum must have arrived home just before us. She's

still dressed in the smart white blouse and black skirt she wears when she is waitressing in 'Coffee & Cake'. Mum likes being a waitress more than her other job as a cleaner, though she moans quite a lot about both. Her dream job, she says, would be working in an art gallery. I'm not quite sure what actual job she would be doing, mind you. She might look arty in her non-work clothes (chiffon scarves, big earrings and voluminous floaty skirts), but she isn't any good at actual art. She made a very slapdash job of painting the skirting boards in the hall.

"Lily! Wake up, girl!" snaps Gran. "Are you going to bring that bag through to the kitchen or are we all supposed to stand in the hall and eat?"

"Sorry, Gran. I'm coming." I run forward and nearly trip over McTavish, our other cat, who has wound himself around my ankles like a furry snake.

The bright, warm kitchen looks clean and tidy, and for a moment I completely forget my troubles. Gran has set the table, made a pot of tea and buttered some thick slices of bread.

"It's like a party," breathes Hudson.

Quipp runs up to me too, his nose quivering at the smell of fish. Both cats purr and press themselves against my legs. I break off two small chunks of haddock and place them in their bowls.

"Here you are. Enjoy," I say, stroking their furry backs. They totally ignore me, intent on nibbling at their salty fish.

"If you two were dogs you would wag your tails to say thank you for that," I scold them. "Cats have no manners."

"I'm starving with hunger!" shouts Bronx, pulling off his boots and skidding across the tiles in his socks.

"No sign of Jenna," says Mum. "She must still be feeling poorly. Run up and ask if she wants some fish and chips, Lil."

My heart thuds in my chest. Mum and Gran will be furious if they find out she's been hanging around town with an older boy when she should be in bed. It'll ruin everyone's dinner if they find out now. Not that I can enjoy it until my sister's safely home.

Before I can think of something to say, the front door bangs and a soaking-wet Jenna rushes in, lured like the cats by the delicious vinegary smell of fish and chips.

"Hi everybody," she says, grinning at us in a weird, un-Jenna-like fashion. "I got the Coke you wanted, Hudson. You moved fast with that buggy, Lil! I'll be back in a sec. I'm just going upstairs to get dry clothes and then I'll tell you how I got on at the doctor. It's a monsoon out there, isn't it?"

Hudson looks bemused, and then pleased that there is

Coke even when he hadn't asked for it. Jenna spins out of the room and rushes up the stairs, boots clattering.

"Why's she so cheerful all of a sudden?" grumbles Gran, always first to smell a rat. "That girl's usually got a face that would sour milk."

"I expect she got good news," says Mum, blithely. "The doctor probably told her there was nothing wrong at all; just growing pains or something."

I'm impressed that Mum remembered that Jenna had a doctor's appointment this afternoon. Gran looks flummoxed for a second, but then recovers her composure and pretends she hadn't forgotten.

"Growing pains, my backside," she snorts, unable to resist the urge to disagree with Mum. "The girl's clearly anaemic. She shouldn't have been out in that weather. Whose daft idea was that?"

She glares at me and I open and close my mouth like a goldfish, flabbergasted by the unfairness of the situation.

Jenna comes back down in a few minutes, hair still damp, but dressed in a dry jumper and jeans. As she slides into her seat opposite me, she puts a finger to her lips. Her eyes are sparkling and she seems to fizz with excitement.

I'm not the only one who notices. Gran's suspicious glare is rather similar to Miss Swanage's.

It turns out, amazingly, that Gran's diagnosis is correct.

The doctor told Jenna she has anaemia, which means she doesn't have enough iron in her blood.

"It's why I've been feeling so tired and breathless," Jenna explains, between mouthfuls of chips. "I told you I wasn't dying, Lil. I look pale because of the lack of iron. And the doctor says that's why I fainted in the middle of geography last week. She says I have to take supplements for a while and eat more iron-rich foods, like eggs and oily fish."

Gran looks exceedingly smug. She adores being right, especially about medical matters. She also adores an opportunity to hint that Mum doesn't feed us a very balanced diet.

"The girls need to have a *proper* breakfast every morning. Cereals and wholemeal bread have iron in them too, you know." She waves her fork at Mum.

"Interfering old busybody," Mum mutters, under her breath. Then adds, in a louder voice, "Jenna is perfectly capable of making her own breakfast. And there's a huge box of Rice Krispies in the cupboard,"

That isn't quite accurate. There's an empty box in the cupboard and a massive, scattered heap of Rice Krispies next to it. But I say nothing. It's best not to wade in when Gran and Mum are narking at each other.

Gran gets stiffly to her feet, folds her arms across her chest and announces her decision. "I'll pop in each morning before Jenna and Lily leave for school and check that they've both had a healthy breakfast. Then I'll give the boys and the baby theirs while you get ready for work. It'll mean an earlier start for me, and I'm not getting any younger, but I can see it'll have to be done."

Jenna rolls her eyes, aghast at the prospect of having Gran about in the mornings too, but I'm delighted. Maybe there will be eggs and bacon sometimes, like she makes when we're staying in the caravan on Millport.

"You don't have to do that, Morag," says Mum, but her shoulders have relaxed a little. I'm sure she'd love to tell Gran to mind her own business, but she knows we could really do with the help.

Gran says no more, sits down and tucks back into her fish and chips. We are all munching away, the silence broken only by Bronx loudly slurping his Coke, when I decide the time is right to enlist adult help in dealing with Jenna.

"Who was that boy I saw you with in the town centre earlier?" I ask her innocently.

Mum's and Gran's eyes swivel towards Jenna.

Jenna glares at me, but I try not to let her fury bother me. Perhaps I'm being an interfering busybody like Gran, but I don't want Jenna hanging around the town centre with Kai Dixon, who smokes, swears, gets in fights, drops

litter and steals stuff. Even if she is raging mad with me –
even if it puts our relationship right back at square one, I
want my sister to be safe.

"Jenna's got a boyfriend! Jenna's got a boyfriend!"
chants Bronx, who's a bit hyper because of the Coke.

Jenna turns on him, her cheeks a fiery red. "Shut up,
maggot. Kai isn't my boyfriend."

Bronx wisely shuts up. I keep talking.

"He put his arm round you," I point out, reasonably.
"Once he'd thrown his cigarette on the pavement."

"Isn't that lovely," says Mum, airily. "Jenna's got a
boyfriend."

I might have known Mum would be no help whatsoever.
She's probably just as scared as I am of Jenna's moods.

Gran isn't. She turns to Jenna, her eyes are shards of ice.
"Who is this person? Smoking? Kai's not a proper name!"
she splutters. "What's his real name? What year's he in at
school? Where does he live?"

"His name *is* Kai, Gran. It's as much a proper name
as Bronx or Hudson." Gran snorts. She doesn't think my
brothers have proper names either.

"His surname's Dixon," continues Jenna. "He's not at
school. He's seventeen. He left at the end of fourth year."

"He was expelled from school for fighting," I murmur.

"He was what!" roars Gran.

"So what does he do now?" says Mum. I can see that she isn't thrilled but she's trying to stay on Jenna's side. "Is he at college? Working?"

"Um, no." Jenna fidgets. "He doesn't want to do any of that kind of thing. He's got other plans."

"Like stealing stuff," I say.

Mum gasps and Gran makes a noise like a trumpeting elephant. Bronx and Hudson stare at Gran, transfixed. I know they would dearly love to copy her elephant noise, but neither of them is daft enough to risk Gran's rage descending on them. It's much more interesting to watch someone else being the target.

"Well, it stops right now, young lady," says Gran. "You've got better things to do with your time than hang around the streets with neds."

Mum nods. Her eyes are worried. "You have Higher Prelims coming up, Jenna."

Jenna's eyes have lost their excited sparkle. They glitter with fury now instead, most of it directed at me. She shoves her plate away and stands up so quickly that her chair topples backwards and dents the freshly painted wall.

"You are such a creepy telltale, Lily," she snarls. Then she turns her back on us and runs upstairs. I feel tears prickling under my eyelids and wipe them away with the back of my hand.

My bag is still sitting in the corner of the room, the note scrunched up inside it. While I help Mum tidy the kitchen after dinner, I keep looking at it, my mind swaying between worrying about the note and fretting about Jenna. I start to feel seasick.

"You're a bit quiet, Lily," says Mum. "Is everything alright? Don't worry about Jenna, love. She's grouchy with everyone nowadays. She'll have forgotten all about it in the morning."

This is so unlikely that I wonder, yet again, if Mum inhabits the same reality as I do.

"Is everything going well at school?" she says, wiping splodges of tomato sauce off the table. "You know I wanted to come to the Meet-the-Teachers evening, but everything's been so hectic with work and the wee ones. Sorry, Lily. Gran said the teachers seem pleased with you. The art teacher thinks you've got real potential, apparently."

"Everything's fine," I say, glancing at my bag. I know I should tell her about the note, but I can imagine what would happen next:

Mum would phone Gran and Gran would storm up to the school, barge into the head teacher's office, threaten to phone the *Largs and Millport Weekly* and get them to run a front-page article about the school's failure to tackle bullying. She would probably also demand that the culprit be tracked down, interrogated under torture, found guilty and hung, drawn and quartered. It would be totally mortifying.

"I'll just go and read the kids their bedtime story and then get on with my science homework," I say, scooping up my bag, then Summer, and backing out of the kitchen. "Bronx, Hudson, wash, brush teeth, put on PJs!"

"It's my turn to choose the story," insists Bronx, as we head upstairs, Summer slung over my shoulder like Santa's sack. "Hudson chose last night."

"I expect you're going to choose *Captain Underpants*, aren't you? And that's what Hudson chose last night. So it doesn't really make a difference who chooses, does it? You both like the same book."

"Yes, but, if Hudson chooses again, it's not fair. It's my turn."

"What about Summer, does she not get a turn?" I ask.

"No, *Captain Underpants* is her favourite too, isn't it, Summer?"

I'm not sure that's true, but she certainly seems happy enough to sit and listen while the boys howl with laughter. By the time I've finished reading in my silly voices, she is nodding off on my knee.

I switch off the boys' light, put Summer to bed, say goodnight and head to my own room. It's pitch-dark outside, so I switch on my lamp and draw my stripy curtains. McTavish is chilling on my duvet. I don't shoo him away as I usually would, but curl up next to his warm furry body. He purrs contentedly and opens one green eye, hardly able to believe his luck.

I don't know why I even attempt to concentrate on my very boring science project. Right now I don't care about the pros and cons of wind turbines. My eyes keep straying to my bag and finally I can bear it no longer. I reach in and pull out the crumpled little note.

In some corner of my brain, where stupidity lurks, I'm hoping that this note will explain everything. But it's just the same. Just as horrible as the first one.

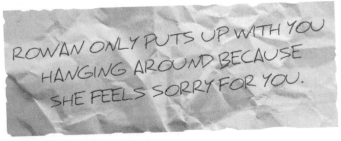

ROWAN ONLY PUTS UP WITH YOU HANGING AROUND BECAUSE SHE FEELS SORRY FOR YOU.

My eyes fill with tears. Is that true? Does she feel sorry for me? Is that why she's always so nice?

Tears dribble down my cheeks and drip off the end of my chin as I scrunch up the note, slip into the bathroom and flush it down the toilet. It's going to be impossible to get the words out of my mind. Every time I see Rowan, I'll be wondering if she's wishing I'd stop bothering her. This is the worst feeling ever.

"I need to find out who is writing the notes," I whisper to the bathroom mirror, wiping the snot and tears off my face. "And make them stop."

When I'm back in my room, I pick up my notebook.

How to find out who's leaving the notes:

 Handwriting analysis.
 Keep a lookout on my locker.

I'm not sure how I'm going to achieve the second one in school corridors patrolled by Mr Diarmid. I need a spy cam, but I'm not sure where to get one.

Suddenly the door crashes open. I jump like a jack-in-the-box. Mac leaps from the bed and hurtles out of the room, tail swishing. Jenna is standing at the door. Her face is distorted with fury. She clearly isn't in a forgiving mood.

"Don't you think you've won, Lily McLean," she hisses. "Don't think for a moment that I'm going to stop going out with Kai just because you've sneaked on me. I hate you, I really do."

The door slams and I'm alone again in my room.

This has been a horrible day, and I'm not just talking about the lousy weather.

Chapter 7

My choice of boyfriend for Jenna:

- Somebody who works hard at school, like Imran.
- Somebody nice looking but not a show-off, like Imran.
- Imran.

The next morning, Jenna ignores me completely. Gran chats away and doles out plates of fried bread, bacon and square sausage, totally oblivious to the frosty atmosphere.

"I'll not be making fry-ups every morning," she declares. "But you should be getting something hot to eat in the autumn. I'll make porridge tomorrow."

Jenna screws up her face in disgust. She hates porridge almost as much as she hates me.

"That will be nice, Gran," I say, helping myself to another rasher of crispy bacon, hardly able to believe my luck.

Jenna rolls her eyes, grabs her school bag and stalks past me, nose in the air. The front door bangs behind her. I pick up my own bag and follow her outside.

"Bye, girls!" shouts Gran cheerily. She's in a good mood because it's dry today and she's planning to hang out some washing in the back garden.

If I ever get excited about stuff like that, kill me.

I chase after Jenna and catch up with her at the traffic lights on Main Street. When I pull at her sleeve, she flinches as if I've burned her arm.

"Listen, Jen, about last night. I wasn't trying to get you into trouble. I just don't want—"

"Shut up, Lily," Jenna interrupts me, her voice a malevolent hiss. "Just leave me alone from now on, will you?"

I watch her march across the road. That makes two people I'm supposed to leave alone. I'll have nobody to talk to by the end of the year at this rate.

When I get to school, I go straight to my locker, unlock it and fling open the door.

A scrap of light blue paper flutters to the ground. I scoop it up. As I'm stuffing it in my pocket, heart thumping, Rowan comes running up to me.

"Where are you off to, Lil? The bell will be ringing soon!"

"I need the loo." I stride towards the girls' toilets and lock myself in a cubicle, terrified that Rowan will read the note over my shoulder. She waits outside, chatting away like a budgie.

"Hurry up, Lil. You're taking ages." She drums on the door with her fingers. "By the way, are you going to audition for a part in *Oliver*? I know you don't like being on stage in front of people, but you have a lovely singing voice. You'd be brilliant as Nancy."

I listen to her cheerful, encouraging voice and then look down at the nasty little note in my hand.

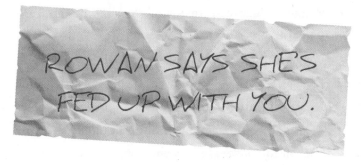

Furious, I rip the paper into a zillion pieces and flush them down the toilet. I lay my head against the cubicle door and give myself a stern lecture.

Somebody is trying to bully me and I'm not going to let that happen. I'm not being anyone's victim. I've known Rowan for years and she doesn't say mean things behind people's backs. Ever. Rowan wouldn't say these things about me. Whoever is sending these notes is telling lies. I'm not going to look in my locker again. It can stay locked. Even if I fall over backwards and end up on YouTube, it will be the lesser of two evils. I'm not going to be dumb enough to be upset by them any more.

I open the cubicle door.

Rowan grabs my arm. Smiling brightly, she pulls me out to the corridor where David and Aisha are waiting for us.

"Lily, at last!" calls Aisha. "Come and save me. David's talking about zombies again."

"I was just pointing out that this school is well equipped to withstand the zombie apocalypse. We've got excellent Wi-Fi and a wide assortment of weapons in the Tech department."

"Well observed, Dave." I smile at him, but it feels fake. "But do you really want to be trapped in the same building as Mr Diarmid and Miss Swanage for umpteen weeks?"

Rowan's still holding my arm. She tugs on my sleeve.

"I meant to ask you, Lily..." she says.

My stomach drops. I eye Rowan warily. She doesn't look as if she is about to give me bad news, but my confidence has taken a big dent recently and I'm not sure of anything at the moment.

"Did you not get my text?"

"When?"

"Last night!"

"No, sorry. My phone's out of charge," I lie. The truth is that I switched it off last night, in case Jenna sent any furious texts. "Ask me what?"

"You know how we always go to Arran for three nights in September... my family and some of my parents' friends? Well, anyway, it's great fun. And... Mum says I can bring a friend this year because we're renting a two-bedroom cottage! Will you come, Lily? David's coming with his mum, aren't you Dave?"

David looks gloomy.

"'Fraid so. It's just me and Mum, because Dad's working. That's his excuse, anyway. I tried to talk Mum into taking me to Menorca instead, since the fares are about the same price and Menorca has sunshine and outdoor swimming pools. But no joy... Arran again, rain or midges, take your pick, sometimes both at once. And endless walks up hills, in the rain, while being attacked by midgies."

"Don't listen to him, Lil!" squeals Rowan, sticking her hand in front of David's mouth. "It will be fantastic; better than Menorca any day."

David removes Rowan's hand. "You're only saying that because Menorca's not an option. I bet if it wasn't for Finn you'd go abroad on holiday like a shot."

"Well, Finn would hate the heat. He's a Canadian Labrador, not a Mexican Chihuahua. I just hope your mum is ok about you coming, Lily, after what happened in Millport."

"I'll ask her tonight," I say. "I'm sure she'll let me go."

I'm totally thrilled Rowan wants me to come, but my family is a big worry. It's only for three nights, though, and Gran will be there to help Mum out… but what about Jenna? What if she gets into some kind of trouble while I'm away? Maybe I should stay at home.

"Are you sure your mum wants me to come?" I ask, full of doubt.

"She likes you, Lily," laughs Rowan. "It was your step-dad she wasn't so keen on. She's quite happy now she knows for sure that he is out of the picture."

"She's not nearly as happy about that as me," I say. I haven't seen my stepfather for months and am hoping I'll never see him again.

I expect my mum is hoping the same thing, especially now that Brian's hanging around. An invasion of flesh-eating zombies would be more welcome at our house than my step-dad.

I smile at Rowan, my bubbly, popular, lovely best friend. "I thought you and I were finished," I say quietly.

"Why on earth would you think that? You and I are

friends for life. You're my bezzie." Rowan laughs and squeezes my hand. "Always."

I haven't lost my best friend. My relief is so great that I let out a long breath, like a punctured balloon. The tightness in my chest releases.

Then I remember Aisha, standing quietly beside us. Rowan said she could bring a friend – just one. Aisha isn't invited to Arran. I feel terrible for her and quickly glance over to see her expression. I'm surprised to see that she is smiling.

"It's ok, Lily. There's no need to worry about me. Rowan explained to me before you arrived that she is only allowed to ask one friend to come, and you guys have been friends forevs," she says amiably. "Anyway, my dad's coming home and I want to spend time with him."

"Oh Aisha, that's fantastic!" I say, giving her a big hug. Her dad has been working abroad for as long as I've known her. "When did you hear?"

"He phoned really early this morning. He said there was some kind of problem with work and he had to stay away much longer than he'd expected to sort things out, but he will be coming home on Friday. I've never seen Mum look so happy!"

Aisha's face is glowing with pleasure. Her beautiful brown eyes sparkle. I suddenly realise how stressed she must have been in the few months we have known her. The bell rings and we head to our classes. I walk to the I.C.T. base with Aisha, who carries on chattering excitedly.

"Imran and Aziz are so thrilled! We're going to decorate the house before Dad arrives; get some light-up balloons from Mapes. I think Imran was worried Dad would never come back. He's such a nerd he's only glad he'll be able to concentrate on his Advanced Higher exams. Did I tell you he wants to study law at Glasgow University? Of course, all Aziz wanted to know was if Dad would be bringing him home a present!"

"My kid brothers are exactly like that. When they find out I might be going to Arran, presents will be the first thing on their minds."

I have a sudden thought.

"Your Imran knows Kai Dixon, doesn't he?"

Aisha screws up her face. "Yeah, but he can't stand him; thinks he's a total ned. Imran says Kai's been telling everyone he's going to break into the school during the September weekend and smash the place up to get revenge for being expelled. Imran says that shows how stupid Kai is, because if anything happens, the police will know exactly who did it."

We walk into the I.C.T. base and sit down at the computers. As always with me, one worry replaces another.

What does Jenna see in Kai Dixon? Why doesn't she go out with Imran instead? He is handsome, sensible, a school prefect and studying hard for his Advanced Highers. He's Mr Perfect.

Telling Mum and Gran about Kai Dixon was a bad idea. It has probably just made Jenna more determined to see him. And if I try and talk to her, to tell her he's planning to break into the school, she'll just go off like a faulty firework.

There must be another way of getting through to her without risking an explosion. But I can't think how.

A buzzing sound comes from my computer. The photograph I'm supposed to be uploading to a document goes pixelated. Stupid machine must be faulty. I stare at the fuzzy image and am reminded again of my little sister haunting me. She was invisible at first, and then slowly the picture became clear.

We've got telepathic powers. I know it worked with Summer in the holidays, so maybe I should keep trying with Jenna? Summer was trying to communicate from another time – speaking to Jenna in the present should be much easier.

Whether she'll listen is another matter. My big sister's not famous for her listening skills.

At lunchtime I sit in the canteen with my friends, chatting about the Arran weekend.

"You'll hate it, Lil," sighs David. "The ferry crossing is fifty-five minutes, much longer than the Millport crossing. Last year I was so seasick I turned as green as Shrek. The waves were mountainous. You know that old movie, *The Perfect Storm*? It was just like that, with waves crashing over the deck and everybody's life in danger, except in the movie everyone dies and we didn't, obviously."

"So it was like a movie where the main character gets on a ferry, feels a bit seasick, and then gets off safely?" Aisha grins. "You'll struggle to sell tickets for that one."

"Don't listen to a word David says," laughs Rowan. "He loves Arran, really. I think climbing Goatfell was your highlight last year, wasn't it, Dave?"

David puts his head in his hands and groans. "I thought I was going to die of exposure or exhaustion or hypothermia. I had massive blisters on both heels. And my brand new Nikes got all muddy and ruined. Thanks for reminding me, Rowan. I had almost blocked it out and now the terrible memory has resurfaced. I'll need therapy when I'm older."

"Stop being such a big drama queen," Rowan chides him. "We'll have a great time. There are loads of lovely walks, we can go swimming at the Auchrannie Leisure Centre or pony trekking or kayaking—"

"Don't be daft, Rowan," interrupts David. "Lily won't be allowed to go if her mum thinks there are any sea-based activities! Sorry, Lily, for mentioning your near-death experience. I expect you'll need therapy too after that trauma. Maybe we'll get two-for-one."

"I won't mention the kayaking to Mum or Gran," I say. "Walking and pony trekking don't sound too dangerous, do they? I'm sure they'll be fine with me doing those sort of activities."

"My mum is bound to have completed risk assessments, anyway," says David. "She's Mrs Uber-Organised. Even on holiday she's still a teacher. It's horrific."

"There's no such thing as a risk-free environment, though, is there?" I say. "I could fall over a paving stone or stab myself with a pencil or die of boredom listening to Mum's friend Brian droning on about trains."

"I don't know why you complain about Brian. He sounds ok to me," says Aisha, fiddling with her phone. "Compared to what you told me about your step-dad, Brian seems quite civilised."

Annoyance surges through me like an electric charge. I told her private stuff about my step-dad's drinking and violence while we alone together on Millport during the summer holidays. She was great about it then, but she sometimes drops hints in front of Rowan and David that she knows stuff about me that they don't. I'm not sure why she does it, but it's pretty irritating.

"Brian does seem a harmless kind of guy," says David, mildly.

"And it must be nice for your mum to have someone to go out with sometimes," adds Rowan.

I can feel myself reddening. Have the three of them been talking about me behind my back? Or am I getting paranoid?

"Well, next time Brian comes over for dinner, I'll invite you all too. You can hear all about how Class 314 trains are used on some peak-time services to Largs. I'm sure you'll be totally riveted." I try to keep the snap from my voice. They haven't ever met Brian. He could be an axe murderer for all they know. And my mum's social life is none of their business.

I stand up so quickly that my chair clatters.

"I'm going to the library. My book's overdue."

The library's busy at lunchtime, but I find a quiet corner by the window. It's the perfect vantage point: I can see Jenna out on the playground, laughing with her friend Sarah. I'm sure it'll help me communicate with her if I can see her and recreate how Summer contacted me. I sit very still and try to focus on my connection to Jenna, remembering one of our trips to Millport with Gran.

We're clambering over rocks and I lose my sandal…
Jenna rescues it using her fishing net. For some reason we
both find the sight of the plastic sandal dangling in the net
hilarious. Gran doesn't seen the funny side at all.

Stay away from Kai Dixon, I think.

Jenna doesn't respond, just keeps chatting away to Sarah.

This isn't working. She can't hear me. I try again.

"Keep away from Kai Dixon!" I say, out loud this time,
forgetting where I am.

My voice rings loud in the library. The librarian tuts and
gives me an impressive death stare through her varifocals.
Danielle and Jade are huddled in a corner at one of the
library's computers and they look over, point and snigger.
I blush, mortified.

But Jenna stops talking, looks around. There's a puzzled
frown on her face. Then she turns back to her friend,
looking so confused I want to burst out laughing.

Instead, I get up and leave the library, a small triumphant
smile on my face.

That evening Jenna doesn't come home for dinner. It's
Gran's bingo night, so she's not around to worry, and Mum
doesn't seem bothered at all.

"She'll be at a friend's house, Lily," she sighs, when I

jump up from the armchair by the window and draw back the curtain for the tenth time.

The weather is drizzly, the street deserted. There's no sign of my big sister.

"Stop being such a worrier. I told you, she'll be at Sarah or Jessica's. Come and watch *Coronation Street*."

"I'll just run a bath for the boys," I say. "They're filthy. I think they've been rolling in mud, like hippos."

"You're a star, Lil," says Mum, reaching for the remote. "Just a shallow bath, mind. The power card needs topping up and we don't want to be left without heating."

Summer is snoozing beside her on the couch, still dressed in one of Gran's horrible hand-knitted jumpers and the blue cord pinafore Mum bought her in the Oxfam shop. She should really be in bed.

"Mum, I've got something to ask you," I say, finally plucking up courage.

Mum stops flicking through the television channels and turns to look at me. "I knew there was something the matter! Is there something wrong at school? Is somebody being unkind to you?"

This is so close to the truth that I'm tempted to blurt out the whole story. It would be a big relief to tell her about the horrible notes in my locker. But I don't. I need to deal with that problem on my own.

"There's nothing wrong, Mum. Something nice has happened. Rowan has asked me to come with her and her parents to Arran for the September weekend. Just for three nights. Is that ok? Please, Mum."

"It's fine with me, Lil. Honestly. I'm really pleased you've been asked. We can't keep you wrapped up in cotton wool, can we?"

"Don't even say that in front of Gran. She'll think the cotton wool is a great plan."

"You're right. She'll head straight to Boots and purchase a bulk order. But don't worry about Gran. It's not her decision, it's mine. And I say yes."

I'm not totally convinced – Gran often ends up having the final say. But at least I'm over the first hurdle. It looks like I might be going to Arran!

Later that evening, I'm reading *War Horse* in my room when I hear the front door slam. Jenna thumps up the stairs, ignoring the fact that there are three little kids asleep in the house. Mum comes storming out of her bedroom and a furious, hissing quarrel begins.

"What time do you call this, Jenna? On a school night, too! Where have you been, young lady?"

"It's not that late, Mum. I was just hanging round the

amusement arcade with Kai. Stop stressing! Leave me alone!"

I switch off my lamp and pull my duvet over my head. This afternoon's efforts in the library clearly haven't convinced Jenna that she's making a terrible mistake by going out with Kai.

My door is flung open.

Jenna stands in the doorway, hands on her hips. "And you! Were you sneaking up behind me in the playground at lunch time? Whispering in my ear?"

"What?" I act shocked. "I was in the library, Jen. Ask anyone."

Jen opens her mouth, as though she's going to speak, then shuts it. She flounces out and I hear her bedroom door slam.

I reach under the bed, rummage around and pull out a heart-shaped cushion. It's purple and fluffy with sequins that spell out the word 'LOVE'. It's not, strictly speaking, my property. I 'borrowed' it from Jenna's room a couple of years ago when I was trying to make my cupboard hide-out under the stairs a more comfortable place to lurk. I think the cushion is hideous, actually, but I can hardly give it back now. And anyway, it reminds me of old times.

When we were younger, Jenna loved that cushion. And back then, she loved me to bits too. If I was feeling sad or unwell, she'd give me her precious cushion and I'd hug it tightly, the way Summer does Roary, the toy lion I gave her. Summer was clutching Roary when she contacted me from the future. It was a connection between us: a gift I'd bought her. Perhaps if I hold Jenna's cushion tightly I will be able to get my feelings across better. It's worth a try.

I grasp the cushion and close my eyes. I can easily picture Jenna storming around her room, throwing clothes and raging after her quarrel with Mum. But thinking about what Jenna's doing right now isn't going to work, is it? I need to think of happy memories. A time when our connection was strong.

I squeeze my eyes tightly shut and let my mind wander back into the past.

Eventually, a picture appears. It's like watching an old movie. I'm about six; gap-toothed, undersized and skinny, my straggly ginger hair pulled back from my face with an elastic band. I'm dressed in a hideous lime dress, clearly one of Mum's bargain purchases. But I'm the happiest girl in the world, squealing with joy and excitement, while my big sister pushes me on the roundabout, faster and faster. Just as I'm beginning to look scared, she leaps aboard, her blonde pigtails flying. We whirl round and round, clutching the bars, shrieking with glee. I'm so light-headed and wobbly that I stumble when I try to clamber off. Jenna grabs me, saving me from falling onto the wet tarmac.

"Super Girl to the rescue!" she shouts and I grin up at her, dizzy and breathless, loving her attention.

I try and hold the picture in my head.

Now, I think. *I'll try and speak to her now.*

"Jenna," I whisper, the sequins on the cushion scratchy against my cheek. "Jenna, can you hear me?"

Nothing. No reply.

"Jenna, I need you to listen. It's important. Can you hear me, Jenna? Kai's dangerous. He's going to get himself into terrible trouble. Keep away from him."

No answer. Zip. Silence, except for the hum of a distant aeroplane as it travels across the night sky and a creak of springs as Mum turns over in her bed.

It's no use. I throw the cushion on the floor, curl up under my duvet and try to sleep. But a single thought keeps crashing around in my head. Jenna heard me whispering in her ear in the playground, and I wasn't there.

Chapter 8

Reasons I don't want to be a teenager:

- Teenagers can't get up in the morning and they waste most of their time lying in bed. Then when they do get up, they're tired. Except late at night, when they stay awake until all hours, so they can't get up in the morning.

- They are moody, and their bad moods outweigh their good moods by about 10 to 1. Everything annoys them, especially parents and younger siblings.

- Sometimes they get spots, and being spotty makes them even grumpier.

Gran is surprisingly unfazed by the prospect of me going away for a few days to Arran. In fact, unlike Jenna, she seems genuinely delighted when we talk about it at breakfast. The boys have gobbled their porridge already and are playing their favourite game: leaping from the fourth step to the bottom of the stairs. Their thuds are alarmingly loud, but nobody's been hurt. Yet.

"Oh, you'll have a lovely time, dear. Arran is gorgeous," she chirps. "Your grandpa and I spent our honeymoon there. I'd never been anywhere so beautiful. I thought I'd died and gone to heaven. Your dad loved Arran too, you know. He was such a keen hill walker. I must get out the photos. They're in an album somewhere. Those were the days when people took proper photographs and put them on display on their mantelpieces or in lovely leather albums. Not like nowadays, when they're hidden away on computers."

Once Gran starts her anti-computer rant, there's no stopping her. According to Gran, if it wasn't for computers and mobile phones, everybody, everywhere, would be sociable and happy and good mannered, like they were in 'her day'. I've never had the nerve to argue with her about it, but I would really like to ask her how all those wars happened in 'her day' when people were apparently so much nicer than they are now.

"So what's Arran like? Is it much bigger than Cumbrae?" I try to steer the subject back to my holiday.

"Oh, it's a much bigger island than Cumbrae. They call Arran 'Scotland in miniature' because it's got everything you could want, from mountains to seaside."

"It's got nothing *I'd* want," snorts Jenna. "It sounds like the most boring place in the world, after Millport. No Subway, no McD's, no Topshop. I bet there's not even a Greggs."

"Well, it doesn't matter if there is or there isn't, because you're not invited, are you?" snaps Gran, who is still miffed about Jenna's refusal to come to Millport during the summer holidays. Gran holds grudges forever.

Jenna's still holding a grudge too. She snarls at me when I ask her to pass the jam.

"Get it yourself, creep."

Gran, who is over at the highchair trying to remove globs of porridge from Summer's hair, whirls round. She picks up a wooden spoon and smacks it against the table. We all jump, except Summer, who picks up her own spoon and starts bashing it against her chair.

"That's quite enough of your language, Jenna McLean. What kind of example is that for the baby?" yells Gran (a bit hypocritically, I think, as I watch Summer crashing her spoon down again and again).

"Bang!" shouts Summer. "Clash, bang!"

"And, by the way," continues Gran, over the din, "I'm babysitting tonight, so make sure you are home from school sharpish. I'll make an early dinner so that you have plenty of study time this evening."

Jenna stands up and grabs her school bag. "I'll be home at four, but I'm going to Sarah's later to practise for our Spanish speaking test. Bye, Gran. See you later."

Jenna dives out of the front door like a torpedo from a warship.

Gran wrestles the spoon out of Summer's hand and then looks at me, eyebrows raised. "Teenagers! Don't you go turning into one of those, Lily."

"Sorry, Gran, but I'm afraid it's only a year away. I promise I'll not metamorphose into a monster overnight."

Gran reaches over and envelops me in one of her big hugs. She smells of Deep Heat and lavender soap. "Right, it's time those boys were dressed. You'd better get going, girl. And don't make promises you might not be able to keep."

All day at school, I think about having a whole weekend with Rowan and David. No chores, no screaming teenagers, no little kids. It's going to be brilliant. I'm so distracted that Mr Barton has to ask me to read aloud from *War Horse*

three times before I hear him. Then it takes me ages to find the correct page because I've been reading ahead and have no idea where everyone else is. Mr Barton isn't too pleased with me, but at least I know what the story's about.

Doug the Thug has no idea. He's too busy annoying Amy Johnson, the poor girl who sits in front of him.

"Mr Barton." She sticks her hand in the air. "Doug keeps poking me in the back with a pencil. It's dead sore."

"Ok, Douglas. Why don't you stop doing that and engage with the text instead, eh? Think about the part Lily just read. Why do you think Joey runs round the paddock, kicking up his heels? How do you think he's feeling?"

Doug thinks hard for a moment, his face screwed up with the effort. "Um, I dunno. It's weird. Is he playing football or something?"

Mr Barton shakes his head sadly. "Douglas, what's the title of this book we have been reading since the beginning of term?"

"Er…" Doug checks the cover. "*War Horse.*"

"Well, there you are, Douglas. Joey is the hero of this book."

"But the book's about a horse."

"Yes, Douglas, Joey is the horse mentioned in the title. He is not a football player, nor is he a weirdo. Joey is a horse, and he is sold to an officer who is heading off to fight during the First World War… hence the title… *War Horse.*"

"Oh, right. That makes sense, I guess." Doug shrugs and goes back to his favourite game of rolling up little pieces of paper and pinging them across the desk.

Mr Barton lets out a very long, sad sigh.

At lunchtime, Aisha tells us some more about her dad's homecoming party, then Rowan chatters non-stop about the arrangements for the weekend.

"We'll pick you up on Friday at four and drive to Ardrossan to catch the five o'clock ferry. It'll be getting a wee bit dark by the time we arrive, which is a shame, but you'll be able to get a proper look at Arran in the morning. We're staying in an old farmhouse outside Brodick, close enough to the town that we can walk there on our own. All the farm's outbuildings have been converted into holiday homes. It's lovely."

"It's perfect if you like florals. Flowery curtains, flowery cushions, flowery wallpaper. Flowery outside, too. It's horrific," grumbles David. "Worst hay fever I've ever had was when we stayed there last year. I sneezed non-stop."

"You'll need to be careful if you ever come round to my house, then, Dave," I say. "You get the full rainforest experience in my garden, including venomous snakes and frogs, probably. Bring your Piriton tablets and blow darts."

"Interesting," says David, his face brightening. "Your garden might be the perfect Endor!"

"What's Endor?" I ask.

David looks at me as if I've asked something unbelievably dumb. This must be how Doug feels when Mr Barton asks him a question in English class.

"Endor is a forested moon, home of the Ewoks. Your garden might be perfect for my Star Wars Lego movie project…"

"Don't let him, Lily," laughs Aisha. "He's planning to make Lego versions of every one of the *Stars Wars* movies. He wants to use the beach near me for Tatooine! We'll never get rid of him."

Everybody laughs. The bell rings and I sigh and pick up my bag.

"Voy a la clase de Español. Adios, amigos!"

I have Spanish while the other three have French, so I won't see them for a while. But just as I'm walking away, Aisha catches up to me and grabs my elbow.

"What's up?" I ask.

Her face reddens. She looks at her feet.

"Lil, I spoke to Imran yesterday about Kai again. Apparently Kai's telling everyone that your big sister is going to help him break into the school on Saturday night."

"What?"

"Imran says he's just showing off and Jenna wouldn't be so daft," Aisha tries to reassure me. "I just thought I should tell you what people are saying. Sorry, Lily."

My heart plummets in my chest. This is worse than I thought – much worse. Not only is Kai Dixon dangerous, but he's pulling Jenna into danger with him.

My mind races as I head to class. Perhaps I shouldn't go to Arran. I shouldn't leave Jenna in Kai's clutches. What if something terrible happens? Jenna may be a bit of a loudmouth – she may skive off sick sometimes, and chew gum in the corridors – but she isn't a criminal. If Kai breaks into the school and Jenna's anywhere near him, she could go to jail.

Tears spring in my eyes. I'm scared for my big sister, and I don't know how to save her.

My stomach twists with worry and I have to pass my locker to get to the Spanish classroom. Seeing it reminds me about my other worry – the nasty notes – and I start to feel sick. To make matters worse, Georgia is leaning against the locker next to mine, laughing with Jade and Danielle.

Silence falls as I walk past. Jade whispers something in Danielle's ear behind me and they fall about laughing again, like cackling hyenas.

I feel my face burning, but I try to keep my head high,

pretend I'm not bothered. Their laughter, the huddled whispers, makes me certain it's them doing the notes. Why else would they be hanging around my locker? They obviously think it's all a hilarious joke, and in a weird way that makes me feel better.

Better because if it's all coming from them, and Rowan has nothing to do with it, then none of it really matters. They're just being stupid and immature and pathetic. Rowan invited *me* to Arran, not them. She wouldn't have chosen me if the notes were true.

Seeing the girls there just makes me more determined to ignore my locker from now on. Georgia must be really jealous of my close friendship with Rowan to do such a horrible thing. Well, I'm not going to let her spoil it. I've got bigger things to think about.

The sick feeling passes, and I'm feeling bizarrely cheerful as I walk home. Practically catching Georgia and the girls red-handed has made me feel less upset. Plus, I've convinced myself that Jenna has inherited just enough common sense from Gran to stay out of trouble.

So the whole way home, instead of worrying, I've been planning which of my clothes are presentable enough to take with me to Arran. My jeans are still fairly decent and

Jenna's fluffy cardigan isn't too hideous. I'll take everything I need in my schoolbag, with the water lily charm Mrs McKenzie gave me at the end of primary school. I had it with me in the summer and it feels like good luck.

I realise suddenly that I've walked right past my own front garden – unsurprisingly, because it's unrecognisable.

The grass has been trimmed, the junk removed, and the flowerbed dug over. I hadn't even realised that a flowerbed existed there. It now looks like a normal front garden: like all the other gardens in the street. Two blue glazed pots filled with winter pansies have been placed at either side of the front door. I stand and stare at them. Either the flower fairies have visited or my Gran has been up to something. David will be gutted. Our garden couldn't look less like a forest moon now.

The door opens and Gran appears, beaming.

"Come in, Lil. I've made a pot of tea."

And she has made pancakes too, which smell delicious and are still warm from the oven. It would all be wonderful, except for the fact that our neighbour Mr Henderson is sitting at the kitchen table, buttering a pancake and slurping tea from one of our chipped mugs. He stuffs the pancake in his mouth like a ten-pence coin in a slot machine.

"Afternoon, Lily," he says, spitting crumbs.

I'm surprised he knows my name. And I'm totally astonished to see him looking so cheerful.

"Hello, Mr Henderson," I say, sidling round him and taking a pancake. I spread it thick with butter and scoff it before it melts all over my fingers.

"Frank has worked a wee miracle in the garden, hasn't he?" says Gran. Her voice is unusually bright, like Jenna's was last night after she'd been with Kai. It's downright eerie.

"He kindly offered to cut the grass before the cold weather sets in, but then he went above and beyond, with the pots and the shrubs. Your mum is going to be thrilled, isn't she Lily?"

I'm not convinced Mum'll even notice, but I nod and take another pancake from the rapidly diminishing stack. Out of the back window I can see that the same transformation has taken place: grass cut, junk removed. Frank has been a busy bee. Maybe he just couldn't stand looking at our overgrown jungle every day. Or maybe he is trying to please Gran. They certainly seem very friendly.

Oh, yuck. Not Gran, too.

"Well, I'd better be going," sighs Mr Henderson. "Thank you for the tea and pancakes, Morag. I've thoroughly enjoyed myself." He gets stiffly to his feet and rubs his back.

Gran showers him with praise.

"It was nothing," he chuckles. "Good to be outside on such a lovely autumn day. *Season of mists and mellow fruitfulness...*"

"*Close bosom friend of the maturing sun...*" continues Gran.

I don't think I can take much more of this. They are reciting poetry. Gran said the word 'bosom'. I think I'm going to be sick.

I take another pancake, smother it in jam and sidle towards the door.

"Oh, Lily," trills Gran. "Brian's coming to the house to pick your mum up soon. They're going out for dinner. Could you make sure the wee ones are clean and the living room is tidy? Thanks, dear."

This is horrendous. They are all pairing off: Mum and Brian, Gran and Frank, Jenna and Kai. Where will that leave me?

Feeling deeply sorry for myself, I go into the living room to clear toys from the floor and plump up the cushions. The room's not nearly as awful as our old one: no damp, peeling wallpaper or stained carpet, no major clutter, yet. It is, however, still full of small children.

Hudson has invited his friend Ryan round to play and they are leaping from the couch to the coffee table and back.

Bronx is sulking in a corner, arms folded across his chest, his bottom lip jutting out. Summer has been dumped in the playpen and is shaking the bars mournfully, like a baby monkey trapped in a cage.

Bronx runs over when he sees me, desperate to tell tales on Hudson.

"Lily! Hudson says we can't make a pirate den because I'll break it!"

"Tell you what, I'll make you all a deal." I put my hands on my hips. "I'll help the three of you to build a really strong, amazing pirate den in your bedroom, *if*, and only if, you go and wash your faces and comb your hair. And clean your fingernails while you're at it. They're filthy."

The three boys run upstairs, shrieking and whooping. I lift Summer out of the horrible playpen.

"Wiwy!" she shrieks, grabbing a handful of my hair.

I carry her upstairs and use an old blanket and cushions to turn the boys' bunk bed into a pirate's den. I even join in the game for a while, just to make sure the boys don't make Summer walk the plank or get eaten by a crocodile.

I can hear Mum rushing around, getting showered and changed.

"Lily!" she yells, through the bedroom door. "Can I borrow your black school tights? Mine are laddered!"

"So are mine, Mum!" I yell back, partly because that

is an actual fact and partly because I only have one half-decent pair left and I need them for school. My other pairs have holes in both toes and more ladders than a snakes-and-ladders board.

When the doorbell rings I carry Summer downstairs, leaving the boys in the den. Clean or not, it's probably best if they stay out of Brian's way. I don't want them mentioning his bald head again or his Mr Twit beard.

Brian's in the kitchen, eating the last pancake.

"Hi, Lily. I've got something for you," he says, looking relieved to see me. No wonder, because Gran is chattering away about her arthritis and Frank's rheumatism. She'll be playing her favourite 'Guess who's dead?' game any minute now.

Brian lifts a book from his battered khaki rucksack. (He carries this rucksack everywhere, as if he's on a permanent camping trip.)

I pop Summer in her seat and take the book from his hands gingerly, as if it's an unexploded grenade.

In fact, it's a glossy hardback called *Birdwatching in Ayrshire and Arran*. I leaf through it and see photographs of some of the seabirds I was sketching this summer on Cumbrae. It's a lovely book and I would really like to have it.

But at that very moment, Jenna walks into the kitchen, sees Brian and rolls her eyes.

If I take the book, she'll think I'm not on her side any more. Disliking Brian is the only thing we've got in common. So I hand it back.

"No thanks, Brian. I'm over birdwatching. It's a bit lame."

Jenna sniggers.

Gran's mouth falls open, but she says nothing. She turns back to the sink and starts clattering dishes, which is scarier than a rant.

Brian takes the book and stuffs it back in his rucksack. He has gone a bit pink. "Your mum said ... I just thought ... doesn't matter..."

I feel really mean. Why did I say birdwatching was lame? Me, who wants to write and illustrate nature books one day.

Mum whirls into the kitchen wearing a floaty purple dress she bought last weekend in the charity shop on Main Street. At least it's long enough to hide the laddered tights. Her long curly hair is tied back with a ribbon and she has a crochet shawl round her shoulders. She looks as if she has chosen her clothes from a dressing-up box.

Brian turns even more pink when he sees her. "Hi, babe. You look fantastic!"

Jenna sniggers again.

"Right, must fly." Mum drags Brian towards the door.

She clearly wants to avoid giving Jenna any more opportunities to be rude to him. She doesn't realise she's too late, and that it's me who has been rude. I feel terrible.

"Bye, Mum, goodbye Brian," I say, trying to make amends. "Have a good time."

Jenna rolls her eyes again and pretends to be sick. I've blown it with her anyway, despite my attempts to make things better between us. I should just have taken the bloomin' book.

Once Mum and Brian have left, Jenna edges towards the door.

"And where do you think you're going, young lady?" says Gran.

"I'm going to Sarah's to study, remember?" Jenna replies, holding out her Spanish folder as if it's a crucial piece of evidence in court. "Sarah's mum says she'll make us pizza, so you don't need to worry about feeding me."

She bolts out of the door, quick as a dog chasing a rabbit, before Gran has managed to open her mouth to argue.

As soon as Jenna leaves, Gran turns on me.

Oh, oh.

I should have bolted too, while I had the chance. I pick up Summer so there's a barrier between me and Gran.

"Lily, I am so disappointed in you!" she barks. "Why on earth couldn't you just take that book when the poor man offered it to you? I have never heard you being bad mannered like that in my life. *Birdwatching is lame*, indeed! You know that's his hobby! What possessed you?"

I sit at the table, hugging Summer close to me, feeling totally alone.

"I don't know," I say sadly. "I wish I hadn't. I'm sorry."

Gran sits opposite me, still glowering.

"If you ask me, which nobody ever does, Brian is good for your mum. He's sensible, sober and steady, like your dad was, God rest his soul. Not like your step-dad. Why she ever took up with him after your poor dad died, I will never understand."

I have never been able to work out what Mum saw in my step-dad either. I think Gran is probably right. Brian doesn't drink alcohol for a start. I know he doesn't because I overheard Mum telling Gran 'Brian's teetotal' and I googled 'teetotal' in case it meant something weird. Then I had to google 'abstinence' because teetotal means 'complete abstinence from all alcoholic beverages.' But, teetotal or not, I still don't want Brian around and neither does Jenna.

To be completely honest I don't want Mum going out with anyone. Not even a mega-famous movie star or a billionaire. I just want everything to stay the same. Our family, no strangers allowed. But everything is changing, whether I like it or not.

"Perhaps Brian's not as bad as my step-dad," I concede. "But Jenna and I think—"

"Don't you listen to that daft sister of yours! Has she had a sensible word to say on any subject under the sun recently?"

Silence.

"Well, has she? You think for yourself, Lily McLean!" Gran wags a finger at me. "Give the poor man a chance. Do you hear me?"

"Yes, Gran."

Chapter 9

My big list of worries:

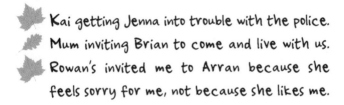

Kai getting Jenna into trouble with the police.
Mum inviting Brian to come and live with us.
Rowan's invited me to Arran because she feels sorry for me, not because she likes me.

That last one's the silliest worry of all, but it's hard to ignore worries. They sneak into your brain.

Later, when the wee ones are in bed and I'm in my room finishing off some art and design homework, I start wondering about contacting Jenna again. I don't believe her story about studying for her Spanish exam with Sarah. She has never shown any enthusiasm for studying in her life, but tonight she couldn't wait to get out of the house.

I put down my notebook, reach under the bed, grab the

fluffy purple cushion and hold it close. I'm going to give this telepathy stuff one more shot.

I begin the same way as before: by closing my eyes.

At first, recalling good memories of Jenna is a bit tricky. The not-so-good ones are much more recent and vivid: her tantrums about not going to Millport, her ignoring me at school, her furious reaction when I told Mum and Gran about Kai. I need to remember further back in time, long before Jenna's metamorphosis into a stroppy teenager, when she was still my smiley, pigtailed big sister.

Eyes closed, remembering, I see a younger me, aged about five or six – freckle-faced and ginger-haired. It's winter and I'm enveloped in a puffy pink jacket two sizes too big and there's a ridiculous woolly hat rammed on my head. Jenna's arms are wrapped tightly around me as she steers our borrowed sledge down the snow-covered slope. Except she can't steer very well, and the sledge is hurtling downhill, out of control. We tumble off, giggling hysterically, and roll like hedgehogs halfway down the hill.

I see it all so clearly: we lie on our backs, side by side, in a deep drift, and Jenna shows me how to make snow angels.

It is only later, as we drag the sledge homeward along the gritty, sludgy pavement, that I start to worry about how our step-dad is going to react when he sees us. Our wet hair and soaking, slush-smeared clothes. I begin to cry.

Jenna understands right away. She hugs me and tells me not to worry.

"Shh, Lil. Stop greetin. I'll tell him it was all my idea. Or... maybe we could go to Gran's house first and dry off in front of her fire? She might even make us a hot chocolate, Lil. Good plan?"

I remember smiling up at her adoringly, tears drying on my red, frost-nipped cheeks. It is a totally brilliant plan.

I keep that picture in my head, like a photograph, and I try to reach my sister.

"Jenna, if you can hear me, say 'yes'," I whisper, hugging the cushion tight.

No answer.

"Jenna, can you hear me?" I say, a little louder. When Summer first tried to contact me, I could hear her voice but I couldn't see her. It was only later that she became visible. I don't need Jenna to see me: I just want her to listen.

All at once my ears are filled with a loud, low-pitched electric drone. A mixture of music and electronic beeping blurs into one disorientating noise. Brilliantly coloured lights flash in front of my eyes.

Scared, I let go of the cushion and the noise fades. The dazzling light dies.

What was that about? It was weird, but familiar too. Slowly it comes to me where I have heard those electronic sounds before, those flashing lights: the big, brash amusement arcade on the promenade!

There's no way Jenna's practising Spanish with Sarah at the arcade. I'll bet she's there with Kai.

Maybe my attempts to contact her are working. Nervously, I pick up the cushion and hug it tightly.

One more time. I squeeze my eyes shut and think again of Jenna and me. We're dragging that sledge towards Gran's house, gleeful at the prospect of hot chocolate.

The cacophony of electronic beeps and loud music starts up again.

"Is that you, Jenna?" I whisper. "Say 'yes' if you can hear me."

Through a haze, I can see my big sister, her dyed-black hair glinting in the bright lights. Jenna is clinging to Kai's arm while he tips coins into an arcade game. She shrieks with delight when the machine's lights flash and coins spill noisily into the metal tray.

"We won!" she yells excitedly.

"*I* won, you mean." Kai scoops up the coins and puts them in his pocket. "I'm going to get myself a beer with all this. Are you coming?"

Jenna's smile slips a bit. She bites her lip, the way she does when she's anxious.

"I can't. I need to get home soon. And even if I did come, they wouldn't let me buy beer. You said we were just going for a walk along the seafront. If I'd known we were coming here, I'd have brought some cash so I could play the machines too."

Kai shrugs. "Well, I'll go to the shops on my own, then. You'd better run along home to Mumsie."

Jenna's lip wobbles, but she doesn't reply. I don't understand why she isn't telling him to get lost. If anyone else spoke to her like that, she would snap right back and storm off.

"Jenna, that guy's a total loser. Come home now!" I say loudly in her ear.

She whips around, eyes wide with surprise, but he grabs her elbow. His fingertips are yellow, the nails filthy, and he's digging them into her arm.

"Hope you're not planning to back out of Saturday night, too," he hisses. "I need you as look out, remember? You wouldn't want me to get caught, would you? I might tell the polis what *you've* been up to…"

"Don't listen to him. He's dangerous!" I'm shouting now, furious that this boy's trying to blackmail my sister.

Jenna tugs herself free of Kai's grip; spins to look behind her again. "Who said that? Lily? Where are you?"

Kai scowls. "Think you're funny, do you? I'm off. See you Saturday."

I take my chance again. "You need to come home now, Jen. Please, Jen." My voice is tight with anxiety.

"Lily?" whispers my sister. "What is happening…?"

Overwhelmed, I loosen my grip on the cushion. The clamour mutes and the lights fizzle and die, like fireworks in the night sky. I'm back in my quiet, cosy bedroom. My heart is thudding and I feel shaky, as if I've got flu.

Unexpectedly, I burst into tears. I throw the cushion so hard that it bounces off the wall and nearly knocks over my lamp. On top of all the other things going on at the moment, this spooky stuff is too much.

Sniffing tearfully, suddenly desperate for company, I tiptoe downstairs and poke my head around the living-room door.

"Do you want a cup of tea, Gran?" I ask.

Gran puts down her knitting needles. She is in the middle of knitting a hideous purple jumper. I hope very much it isn't my Christmas present. Maybe it's for Jenna, to match the purple streaks in her hair. She will freak when she sees it.

"I thought you'd gone to bed. That would be lovely, dear. Are you alright, Lil? Your eyes are all red."

"I'm just tired, Gran. I've been working really hard on my homework," I say. *Unlike Jenna, who's definitely not studying with Sarah, but hanging out with Kai in the amusement arcade.*

Telling Mum and Gran about Kai made Jenna so mad at me that I am reluctant to make things even worse by telling Gran the rest. And anyway, I can hardly announce to Gran that I've been communicating telepathically with Jenna. She'll think I've lost the plot.

I make two cups of strong tea and then come and sit beside her on the sagging couch.

"You sure you're ok, Lily?" she says, with a worried frown. "I hope you're not coming down with something. Moira Benson's wee grandson has a terrible dose of the chicken pox. He's demented with the itching, poor wee—"

"I've definitely not got chicken pox, Gran," I laugh. "I had that when I was at nursery, remember? I was playing an angel in the Nativity play and you wouldn't let me go because I was covered in itchy scabs. I was totally devastated but you said I would probably be an angel next year. So I waited and waited until the following Christmas and then they gave me the part of the bloomin' donkey!"

"Oh, aye, I remember now. You were the sulkiest donkey ever to appear on a stage. Face like fizz, even though I'd made you a lovely grey wool hood with long ears. So if it's not chicken pox…" Gran wracks her brains to think of a possible disease to fit my symptoms.

"Honestly, Gran, There's nothing wrong with me.

I'm fine." I'm getting a bit tired of hearing myself tell everyone I'm fine when I'm not, but the truth is so complicated.

Gran takes a packet of Hobnobs out of her bag and we sit together, dunking the biscuits in our tea. I've just finished mine when the front door bangs open. Jenna comes storming into the living room, flings her folder on the coffee table and points at me.

"What were you doing in town tonight?" she yells. "Why were you spying on me?"

"Calm down, young lady," snaps Gran. "Lily has been here all evening. She hasn't left the house. And what may I ask were you doing in town? You told me you were studying at Sarah's house!"

Jenna looks flustered. "I was. We just popped out for five minutes when we'd finished. I'm allowed a life, aren't I?"

"You get more freedom than I would allow you, madam. When I was your age I had real responsibilities. I was expected to help my mother in the house and hold down a full-time job in Coats Thread Mill."

Jen and I have heard this lecture a lot. In fact, we've heard it so often that we can repeat it word-for-word. Back when she was still speaking to me, Jenna told me that if Gran did the 'I had real responsibilities' speech one more time, she'd go ballistic.

"I'm glad you're home, Jen," I break in, before Jenna goes ballistic. "Did you get a lot of studying done? I like it when Rowan and I study together. I think I remember stuff better when I discuss it with someone else. Don't you?"

Jenna's lips tighten and her eyes narrow. She is giving me the same suspicious glare that I got from my P.E. teacher, Miss Swanage. I can tell she's sure she heard me speak to her in the amusement arcade. But she also realises that I can't have been anywhere near her, so she is now wondering if she is going mad and hearing voices. I can tell, because it's how I felt when it happened to me.

But I'm offering her an escape route from Gran's interrogation, so she takes it. My sister's not stupid.

"Yeah, we got on well. I'm feeling a lot more confident about the speaking test. But it was tiring. I'm off to bed. Night, Gran. Night, Lil."

I give her a few moments and then go up to bed too, my head buzzing. I can't seem to make up my mind what to do about Jenna. One minute I'm sneaking on her, the next I'm trying to cover for her.

It takes a while before I realise what has happened.

Jenna came home! She must have left the arcade almost immediately after I spoke to her, rather than following Kai. This telepathy business is actually working.

The question is: will the cushion fit in my rucksack, because I might need it on Saturday night to save my big sister from disaster.

Chapter 10

The list of note-writing non-suspects:

🍁 It obviously isn't Rowan, David or Aisha, because they like me and the person who is writing these notes clearly doesn't.

🍁 It isn't Cheryl. I'm not being mean, but if it was her, the notes would look something like this:

> rOVAN SES YOO SHUD
> LEEV HUr ALOAN.

🍁 In Georgia's gang, it's unlikely to be Jade. She is so obsessed with her own appearance that I don't think she has even registered my existence. And if she did, she's more likely to offer me a 60 Minute Makeover than sneak nasty notes into my locker.

Jade's friends, on the other hand, are now my prime suspects, especially since I saw them loitering and giggling around my locker. I can see why Georgia and Danielle might be troubled by my close friendship with Rowan. They want Rowan in their gang – who wouldn't? But I'm in the way, so they need to get rid of me. Georgia often ignores my presence so blatantly that I feel I must be invisible. She's my number-one suspect.

Danielle is my number two, because she always tries to be exactly like Georgia, even when Georgia's being horrible. Danielle is a bit of a sheep, though, and I can't imagine her writing and delivering the notes on her own. Perhaps they've hatched this plan together. Maybe I should've held on to the notes, like Miss Swanage did to me, for 'evidence gathering'. I can hardly do handwriting analysis without them. Some detective I'd make.

Because it's the last day before the September weekend, Thursday at school is a dress-as-you-please day. These are always tricky, but I manage to find a cleanish t-shirt and wear it with my black school skirt. I'm keeping my good clothes for the September weekend. David wears jeans and a t-shirt, but has added a black cloak, lightsaber and Darth Vader helmet.

"Lose the helmet, Dave," says Mr Barton, as he hands out photocopies of 'Anthem for Doomed Youth'.

"But it's supposed to be a dress-as-you-please day, sir," David grumbles while I help him tug the plastic contraption off his head.

"You are welcome to wear it during your lunch break." Mr Barton grins. "We are all looking forward to watching you try to eat while wearing a full face mask, aren't we? But I think you'll agree, David, that Darth Vader's heavy breathing isn't at all appropriate for reciting Wilfred Owen's beautiful war poetry... perhaps even disrespectful?"

David stuffs the mask into his bag. It doesn't make another appearance, though he swishes round the school in his black cloak all day, brandishing his light sabre, until that's confiscated during double history.

"Are you coming on the Arran ferry dressed as Darth Vader?" asks Rowan, when the home-time bell rings.

"Maybe," says David. "Though the weight of the cloak might impede my survival prospects if the ferry capsizes. And your father will give you that look that says 'Rowan, that friend of yours is a proper weirdo.'"

It's such a good impression of Rowan's dad that we all fall about laughing.

"Oh, Dad's used to you by now, Dave," says Rowan. "That's not the problem. It's just that if you are planning to wear that cloak, I would get your weaponry back from the history department first. Without the mask and lightsaber, you look more like Ron Weasley heading to the Yule Ball in his dress robes, and I'm not sure that's the look you're after."

Aisha snorts with laughter. "I'm going to miss you guys. But I can't wait to spend some time with Dad. He's promised to take Aziz and me over to Edinburgh on the train to visit our grandparents too. It's going to be brilliant, as long as Aziz stays out of my way."

"That'll be tricky on a train," I say. "You might need to lock him up in the guard's van."

"Or you could tie him to the railway tracks," suggests David. "But that's probably going a bit far."

"He *is* the most annoying kid brother in the universe," Aisha sighs. "I don't think tying him to a rocket and sending him off into space would be going far enough."

"You obviously haven't spent enough time with Bronx and Hudson," I add.

Aisha turns and gives me an unexpected hug.

"Have a good time on Arran, Lily," she whispers in

my ear. "I'll miss you such a lot. You're my best friend ever. I mean it."

"I'll miss you too, Aisha." I hug her back. I don't add anything about her being *my* best friend, though, because that wouldn't be totally accurate. Rowan's my very best friend in the world and David is the only boy friend I need. Aisha is a brand-new friend. I only met her a few months ago and we're really still getting to know each other.

"I hope you have a great time with your dad," I say instead, because I really do hope her weekend goes well. She has missed her dad so much and it's lovely to see her so sparkly.

I rush home, excited and happy about the prospect of the weekend away. When I reach the house I charge through the door, fling my bag on the kitchen floor and swing Summer up into the air.

"Freeeeeedom!" I yell. "No school for four days!"

"Put that wean down!" snaps Gran. "She's just drunk a big cup of juice. She'll be throwing it up all over you!"

I put Summer down and she toddles after Quipp, who hisses and darts through the cat flap to safety. There's half a loaf of bread left, so I pop a couple of slices in the toaster.

Gran doesn't seem quite as thrilled as I am about the prospect of a long weekend. I'd forgotten it means that she'll have the boys at home for two extra days. Mum will still have to work as usual, and I won't be around to help keep the boys occupied.

As if on cue, there's a sudden ear-splitting scream from the living room as war breaks out again between Bronx and Hudson.

"If I were a rich woman, I'd send that pair to boarding school," Gran mutters darkly. "I might even 'forget' to pick them up during the holidays."

"Gran, that's not very kind," I say, crunching on my buttery toast.

"Och, you know I'm only joking," chuckles Gran. "They're both perfectly adorable … when they're sleeping."

Hudson and Bronx choose that moment to charge into the kitchen, screaming abuse at each other. The boys aren't exactly helping their case here.

"Hi boys, I'm making you some toast." It's easy to divert their attention with food. "Would you like jam or just butter?"

"Jam, please. Lil, Bronx hit me! It's sore! My arm's breaked!"

"You wouldn't be able to wave it around like that if it was broken. Give it a rub and it'll be fine." I turn from one snivelling boy to the other. "Bronx, what did you do hit Hudson for? You promised me you would never do that again!"

"Yes, but Lil! He says that I won't get presents for Christmas! He says Santa's elves don't know where I live any more!"

Gran towers over them, hands folded across her chest. "Santa knows exactly where you live. He's up there in the North Pole listening to the pair of you screeching and fighting like two cats. He is probably putting you on the Naughty List right now."

Bronx's bottom lip wobbles. This could end badly. I step between Gran and the boys.

"I think Santa gives warning cards first, like they do at school."

The boys gawp at me. Bronx doesn't look totally convinced.

"So, remember to behave really well this weekend, just in case. You don't want to get a warning card."

There, I've done my bit.

"But Lily, even if I'm really, really good, Santa might get it wrong!" wails Bronx. "And an old lady lives in our old house. She won't want a tablet or a Nerf gun."

"Two Nerf guns!" squeals Hudson. "I want one too! And a Lego Batmobile, and—"

"Christmas is months away, you dopes." I pass them each a slice of toast and jam. "We'll write a letter to Santa much nearer the time with our new address written at the top, just to be sure. But Bronx, tablets are expensive. Santa might not have—"

"If he wants tablet for Christmas, I can make it easily enough," interrupts Gran. "Although it's pure sugar. He'll be hyper all day."

"No, Gran, he doesn't mean… oh never mind."

There's a knock at the back door. Gran flings it open to reveal Mr Henderson standing on the step. He's carrying a big tray of plants and he's grinning like a garden gnome.

"Afternoon, Morag. I've brought marigolds to brighten up the beds," he says. "Maybe I should have brought lilies, eh, with young Lily being here."

Gran shakes her head. "Och, no. Lilies are for funerals. Marigolds are much cheerier."

Thanks, Gran. Charming.

"I'm very grateful I didn't get lumbered with Marigold for a name," I mutter.

"I've been meaning to ask, Morag," says Mr Henderson, pulling off his woolly hat. "There's a tea dance at the hotel next month. I was wondering if you'd care to accompany me?"

I cringe so hard I think my face might break. There can be no situation more awkward than watching your gran being asked out on a date. Could he not have waited until I was out the room? Out the house? In another galaxy, far, far away?

While Gran flusters I make my excuses. "Um, I'm going to go and get myself organised for tomorrow. Don't drip jam on the floor, boys."

I run upstairs to empty my schoolbag. The cushion is going to take up a lot of space but I'm determined to bring it. If Kai really is planning on trashing the school on Saturday night, I need to stop Jenna from joining him.

But first, I need to wash my hair and make myself look presentable to Rowan's parents. I head for the shower, but Jenna has beaten me to it, so I trail back into my room and wait for her to come out.

Eventually her bedroom door slams and I try again. The bathroom floor is slick wet, the air steamy, and a towel has been flung in a corner. As I close the door behind me, I notice a very fancy bottle of shampoo lying in the base of the shower. It doesn't look like one of Mum's usual budget purchases. I reach in, pick it up and flick open the lid. It smells of expensive and exotic things, like aloe vera and ylang-ylang, whatever they are. I'm right: it's very expensive, according to the label on the lid.

Suddenly, Jenna crashes into the room, hair dripping wet. She barges past me and plucks it out of my hand. "That's mine!"

"It can't be, Jenna! You don't have that sort of money..." A horrible thought seizes me. "Wait – did you steal it?"

"Don't be stupid," she retorts, but she blushes and her hand goes up to her mouth. The way it always does when she's fibbing. She rushes back to her bedroom, clutching her towel around her, the bottle safely in her hand

I shouldn't go to Arran at all, I think, as I wash my hair with a dribble of green gunk from Mum's economy-sized bottle of supermarket own-brand shampoo.

And then it dawns on me. Kai's threats to tell the police on Jenna make sense now. She'll be so scared he'll dob her in for stealing, she'll let him talk her into doing even more dangerous stuff. Like breaking into the school. Theft, vandalism, burglary… how many years might she get?

Rubbing at my stinging eyes, I step out of the shower and try to dry myself with the wet towel from the floor. I gaze at my reflection in the steamy mirror. I know I should stay at home.

Chapter 11

Things I would like to bring to Arran in my backpack if it wasn't being taken up with Jenna's silly 'LOVE' cushion:

- Cold hard cash (if only I wasn't skint).
- Warm fleecy pyjamas, because nights on Millport are chilly, so I'm guessing it's the same on Arran.
- A new toothbrush. One with tunes and multi-coloured lights.

It's Friday, and I've packed and re-packed my bag a zillion times. Last night I decided to stay at home for Jenna, but today I've changed my mind: I'm going to Arran. It *is* possible to be in two places at once. I just need more practice.

Packing is not any fun. My pyjamas are an embarrassment. So is my toothbrush. I wish I owned the cosy red-checked PJs I saw on Largs High Street last week. My current ones are Jenna's babyish pink cast-offs, two sizes too small – they barely reach my knees. And the bristles on my old toothbrush are flattened like a Siberian forest hit by an asteroid. David's toothbrush is shaped like a Star Wars lightsaber and has flashing lights. It might be a bit nerdy but it would make brushing my teeth more entertaining.

And my financial situation is bad. I have £1.39 and I only have that much because I 'discovered' a pound coin down the back of the couch. (I also found two sticky sweet wrappers, three marbles, two Lego blocks and lots of fluff, but they're not coming with me to Arran.)

The most important item is the hideous sequined 'LOVE' cushion, because it will help me stay in touch with my big sister while I'm off gallivanting in Arran. I need to keep an eye on her, whether she likes it or not.

I'm a hundred per cent certain that she won't like it one bit.

It's 4:03pm. I am standing at the front window, hopping from one foot to another, while Bronx and Hudson quarrel over which cartoon they are going to watch next. They roll on the ground like puppies, yelping and scratching. Then they try to drag me into the argument, but I'm much too distracted to care.

"Lily! Tell him it's my turn! He won't give me the remote!"

"What does it matter?" I snap. "You've watched every single one of those stupid cartoons five hundred times before. They're all equally dumb. Why don't you read a book or something instead?"

Bronx has Hudson in an armlock, but he looks up at me, eyes wide with horror, as if I'd just suggested they go and play on the motorway. He loves it when I read him stories, but reading a book on his own is way too much like hard work.

"Why are you so grumpy, Lily?" Hudson wriggles out from Bronx's wrestling hold, his face creased with concern. "You sound like Jenna!"

"I'm not grumpy. I'm totally fine," I lie.

I turn back to the window, tears pricking my eyelids. My worries about Jenna are making everything else seem ten times worse. Rowan's three-and-a-half minutes late. Four minutes. What if they've forgotten to come and get me? What if I've made a mistake and was meant to meet Rowan at the ferry port in Ardrossan?

But then I see her dad's black jeep turning into our road. They haven't forgotten me.

"Gran! Mum! Rowan's here!" I run into the kitchen to say goodbye.

Mum's just come in from work and is sitting with her feet up on a chair, looking frazzled.

"That's great, Lily!" she says cheerfully, although I can see a tiny flicker of panic in her eyes. "Oh, I'll miss you, sweetheart."

"Have a lovely weekend, dear," says Gran, pressing a ten-pound note into my hand. "Take good care of yourself. Don't forget to stay well away from the water. I couldn't cope with another dose of heart failure."

"Staying away from water will be a little bit tricky on the ferry, Gran," I laugh. "But I promise not to go near the railings and I definitely won't be going swimming. The sea will be baltic."

"Have a wonderful time, Lily!" Mum gets up and gives me a big hug (but no cash, sadly).

I know how ungrateful that sounds, but I'm a little worried that I'll be expected to pay for my own ferry fare and meals. Ten pounds, or £11.39 to be absolutely precise, isn't really going to cover stuff like that, is it?

Summer toddles over and grabs me round the knees.

"Me an' Woawy come wif Wiwy!" she wails.

"'Fraid not, Summer," I say, pulling gently away. "I need

to go. That's Rowan's dad blasting his horn. Bye everyone. See you on Monday!"

Quarrel forgotten, Bronx and Hudson rush into the kitchen and wrap their arms round my middle. They are clearly after something.

"You're our favouristist sister in the whole wide world," says Hudson, looking up at me with wide grey eyes, his long dark eyelashes fluttering. "Will you get me a present while you're away, Lily?"

"Yup, you're the best, Lily," agrees Bronx, smiling innocently. "So, can you get me a new water pistol please? Hudson broke the one you bought me in Millport."

"It wasn't my fault!" Hudson instantly forgets all about looking angelic. "Bronx left it lying on the path! And then he was so mad when I stood on it by mistake that he stamped on mine on total purpose!"

"Sorry, 'fraid not, boys. No water pistols this time." I hug them back. "I'm only going away for three nights. No time for shopping. And I really need to go. Be good!"

Before I leave, I shout goodbye to Jenna, but there's no reply from her room, just the thumping sound of dance music.

"Take care, Jenna," I whisper. "Stay safe."

I hurry out the house, swinging my bag, trying not to feel guilty about leaving them all. It will be great to get away. I'll be back really soon, and I'll be there for Jenna on Saturday night.

Rowan's dad is in the driving seat, smiling cheerily. Her mum is in the front passenger seat, gesturing at me to hurry.

"Come on, dear," she calls. "We're running a little late, and we don't want to miss the ferry."

So far, so normal. Rowan's mum is always fussing. But as I approach the big car, my steps slow. I rub at my eyes with my free hand, hardly able to believe what I'm seeing.

Instead of sitting behind her mum, Rowan is squashed right at the back of the seven-seater jeep beside her dog, Finn. And perched in the centre of the car, looking bored and irritable, sits Georgia.

Her mother, who I've never officially met but have seen and heard at school parent's nights, is beside her. She looks very glamorous in a fur-trimmed coat. But all I can focus on is the girl who is trying to steal my best friend.

Totally horrified, I have to fight the urge to start walking backwards. I don't want to go to Arran now. I want to stay safely at home. Why didn't Rowan tell me Georgia was coming too? We've never talked about it, but she can't be totally unaware that Georgia thinks I'm a particularly unattractive species of insect, like a cockroach or a maggot.

"Come on, Lily! What on earth's the matter?" shouts Rowan's mum. "Gordon, go and help with her bag!"

Rowan's dad leaps out of the car and takes my schoolbag. "In you pop," he says heartily, opening up the boot. "Wow, this bag weighs a ton. Have you packed for a fortnight?"

I smile weakly at his joke. My bag is mostly purple cushion, and weighs very little. I jump up beside Rowan, force myself to smile at her and concentrate on patting Finn, who quivers with delight and slaps his heavy tail against the pile of cases. At least I'm not squeezed in between Georgia and her mother.

Georgia stares ahead, not even acknowledging my mumbled greeting.

Her mother is staring out of the car window at the terrace of local authority houses, gasping in astonishment. It's as if she's an astronaut who has just crash-landed on an alien planet. She reaches forward and taps Rowan's mother on the shoulder.

"I don't think this looks a very salubrious street," she says sharply. "I would tell Gordon to drive off quickly, before some urchin appears and steals your tyres."

I feel my face blush scarlet. I open my mouth to make some kind of crushing retort, but no sound comes out. I'm such a wimp. If only my gran was here with me.

She has no time for people who think they're better than others. I imagine Gran bristling with annoyance, stage-whispering criticisms like there's no tomorrow. She might even brandish her handbag like a weapon. Perhaps it's good that Gran's not here.

"It's a perfectly nice street!" says Rowan hotly, leaning over the back seat. "Mr Henderson is Grandad's bowls partner, and he lives next door to Lily. Doesn't he, Mum?"

"Yes, dear, I believe he does. Fi, you really are a ghastly snob sometimes!" Rowan's mum laughs, as if being a ghastly snob is quite a fun thing to be.

Georgia's mum laughs too, a deep, throaty laugh, and tosses her hair, all glossy streaks of caramel and honey. She clearly doesn't care that she has just been incredibly rude. This is shaping up to be the worst weekend ever and we're not even on the ferry yet.

Rowan squeezes my hand and beams at me. "Don't pay any attention to Fiona," she whispers. "She's always like this. Last year she told me I was getting podgy!"

Perhaps Rowan presumed I knew Georgia would be coming along. After all, Rowan and David's families have been going to Arran with their friends in September for as long as I've known them. I just hadn't realised that Georgia's mother was one of those friends. If I'd thought for a moment Georgia was coming with us, I'd have made an excuse not to go. I can just imagine her mocking reaction when she sees my shrunken pink pyjamas and my scruffy old toothbrush. I'm doomed.

Rowan, on the other hand, is fizzing with excitement and chattering away about all the fun we're going to have in Arran. Even Georgia starts to thaw in the warmth of her enthusiasm.

"If the weather's not too wet, let's go for a picnic tomorrow at the lochan!" Georgia turns round to grin at Rowan.

"Oh yes. Going on walks with Dave is always a laugh. Remember, Lily, I told you that David nearly had hysterics over the state of his trainers when we climbed up Goatfell?"

I remember. But I don't recall her mentioning that Georgia was there too.

"And then he lost one in that bog!" laughs Georgia. "He was hopping around for ages and we couldn't help him because we were too busy laughing. It was hilarious!"

"Georgia, must you prattle right in my ear? You're giving me a migraine," hisses Fiona.

Georgia flushes and then sits, stony-faced, gazing out of the window for the rest of the journey.

No wonder Georgia's so snarky with people, with a mother like that. I close my eyes and picture my own mum, smiling good-naturedly, her long tangled hair falling into her eyes. Fiona and Georgia would sneer at everything about my mum: her accent, her job, her eccentric clothes. But my mum would never tell me to shut up like that.

At last, we reach the ferry terminal at Ardrossan. The sky is darkening and from the car window I can see leaden-grey water. Suddenly the memory of Millport comes flooding back: falling in, floundering helplessly, screaming as waves wash over me, my nose and mouth filling with icy salt water. A shudder goes right through my body. The giant ferry is rocking back and forth, pushed by the churning waves. I don't want to get on board. I'd much rather stay safely on dry land.

Gran isn't the only one who has been shaken up by my accident in the summer. Rowan understands immediately. She squeezes my hand and gives me a comforting hug. After all, she was there too, as were David and Aisha, on that terrible night on Millport pier. My friends must have been petrified as they battled to save my life. This weekend can't be that bad if I've got two of them with me.

"Everything's ok, Lil." Rowan smiles at me. "It's a big boat and you're not in any danger. You're quite safe, I promise."

Ten minutes later, we're aboard the ferry and climbing the steps to the upstairs lounge. Poor Finn has been left behind in the car.

It's nothing like the tiny Millport ferry. There's a café,

for a start. Rowan's dad buys coffees for the adults and frothy hot chocolates for Rowan, Georgia and me. I offer to pay for mine, but he tells me not to be silly, it's his treat. I'm not sorry, as paying for it would have taken a big chunk out of my funds, but I'm glad I offered. Fiona and Georgia take theirs without even saying thank you.

"Oh, yuck, Gordon, this coffee's like dishwater!" Fiona pulls a face. She seems to be able to say whatever she wants and get away with it.

I can imagine what my gran would say if I complained like that. *Your coffee's like dishwater, is it indeed? Well, I've got a sink full of dirty dishes you can start washing right now!*

I miss Gran already, and we're not even on Arran yet.

We're sitting round a table in the busy café, sipping our drinks, when I see David striding towards us, black cloak swirling, light sabre tucked into his belt, Darth Vader helmet under one arm. An elderly man gawps at him, shaking his head in disbelief.

"Wow," mutters Georgia. "What did I do to deserve this?"

Fiona raises her eyebrows. "What are you mumbling about, Georgia. Speak up, for goodness' sake!" She turns to see what her daughter's staring at and gasps. "What on earth is that eccentric child wearing now? He looks *ridiculous.*"

"Dave's a major Star Wars fan." Rowan leaps to David's defence. "He's the Jedi Knight of Star Wars fans."

David arrives at our table and grins amiably at us. He doesn't seem at all bothered by Fiona's sour expression.

"Mum's on her way up." He slides onto the bench beside me. "She's checking her inventory for the umpteenth time. She needs to be sure we've brought sufficient emergency socks and enough bandages to wrap an Egyptian mummy. Otherwise, the whole civilised world will collapse into anarchy."

"I hope you've brought more conventional clothing," says Fiona. "I absolutely refuse to walk around Arran with you in fancy dress."

"No worries, Mrs C," says David cheerfully. "All my clothes are totally suitable for Star Wars conventions. Is that what you mean by 'conventional'?"

Luckily, before Fiona can reply, David's mum arrives and steers the conversation on to safer topics, like the weekend weather forecast (reasonable) and today's news headlines (bad).

The ferry lurches, buffeted by the fierce wind and high waves. The hot chocolate sloshes in my stomach and I think I might be about to sick it back up. I sit as still as I can and fix a smile upon my face while the others chat. Despite my moment of optimism earlier, I can't help worrying that a whole weekend in the company of Georgia and her mother isn't going to be one bit fun.

"Are you feeling alright, Lil?" asks Rowan. "You've gone a horrible green colour."

"I'm just going to get some fresh air," I mutter. "I'll be back in a second. 'Scuse me, Dave."

I leap up and hurry towards the door leading to the deck.

Outside, a freezing wind blows full in my face. I lean against the railings, eyes squeezed shut, gulping air. I've no intention of looking down into that black, glistening water, but I can still hear the waves smashing against the sides of the ferry. The awful memory of struggling in freezing water, gargling and choking, sinking under the weight of my sodden clothes, floats to the surface of my mind again.

"It'll all be over soon," says a cheerful voice. "We could stand right at the front of the boat, hold out our arms and re-enact that scene from the old *Titanic* movie if you like, though we might not want to tempt fate on a cold night like this. There may be icebergs."

"Um, no thanks, David. I'll give that a miss. I just needed some air, though I'm getting a bit more than I bargained for out here." I turn and wag an accusing finger. "You should have told me."

"I know. I've been feeling bad about it. But would you have come to Arran if you knew Georgia would be here?"

I shake my head.

"Well, I wanted you to come. So I failed to mention the fact she and her mum were coming too. Was that a bit selfish of me?"

"Just a bit. But then I do owe you my life, so I guess I need to let it go."

"I was going to bring that up if you got angry with me, believe me."

A big wave crashes against the bow, and I shiver.

"You're going to get hypothermia out here. Come back inside, you eejit. Your mum and gran will murder Rowan and me if we don't return you in one piece."

"I'm fine," I lie, once again.

Chapter 12

Things I discover on my first night in Arran:

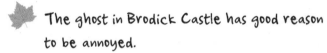

The ghost in Brodick Castle has good reason to be annoyed.

Napkin rings are actual things.

Truth or dare is my least favourite game ever.

When the car rattles over the ramps that lead from the ferry to the pier, I let out a long breath. I feel quite light-headed with relief now that we are on solid ground. The tingling feelings of excitement begin to return. I'm here on Arran with my two best friends for a whole weekend!

"That's Brodick, Arran's main town," explains Rowan, pointing out of the car window. "We'll go there tomorrow or on Sunday morning before we go home. Brodick Castle has its own ghost called the Grey Lady. She was tossed in the dungeons because she caught the plague – and then she died of starvation. The poor woman… it's no wonder she decided to come back and haunt the castle, is it?"

"It kind of serves them right," I agree.

"We don't need a guidebook when Rowan's around, do we?" says Fiona, in a mocking tone that reminds me very much of Georgia.

It is beginning to get dark, but the town is brightly lit: a long meandering line of shops, cafés and restaurants separated from the beach by a wide road. We turn left, out of town, drive along a short stretch of coast road and then down a bumpy farm track. The farmhouse is long and low, whitewashed and lit with Christmassy white fairy lights. It's beautiful. The other buildings nestle around it.

When Rowan's dad pulls to a halt, Finn, Rowan and I tumble out of the back of the car. I grab my holdall and she pulls out her trolley case. Finn starts sniffing the ground, as if he's searching for clues.

"We're staying over there with Mum and Dad," says Rowan, pointing at a tiny detached cottage at the far side of the courtyard. "The others are in the main farmhouse."

That's the first piece of good news I've had so far. At least Georgia won't see me in my tatty, too-small pink pyjamas.

"Oh, my spine is agony!" wails Fiona, as she collects her luggage from the boot. "I felt every bump on that road. Come along, Georgia, help me with this heavy case, for goodness' sake."

Fiona swans up to the front door of the farmhouse and lets herself in. Georgia trails along behind her, dragging their cases. The door slams behind them.

David's mother pulls a face. Looks like I'm not the only one who isn't too keen on Fiona.

Rowan pulls me towards the cottage, anxious to show me where we'll be staying for the next three nights. Finn follows close behind, his tail wagging, delighted to have a new place to explore.

David wasn't wrong about the flowery décor. The living room wallpaper has enormous pink roses, like an explosion in a florist's shop. Rowan leads me upstairs to show me our room. It's quaint, with a large dormer window, two white metal bedsteads covered in flowery duvets and bare floorboards brightened by a sheepskin rug. It's really pretty. Rowan heaves her trolley case up on to the bed and pulls out a floral Cath Kidston washbag.

"If you can't beat them, join them!" She waves the washbag at me. "I've brought flowery PJs too. Look. Mum bought them in John Lewis. Sweet, aren't they?"

"They're lovely," I say. "Shame I haven't got anything

floral with me. I should have picked some of Mr Henderson's new flowers and worn them in my hair."

I put my own bag on the other bed. And then I see it, caught in the zip of the small side compartment: a tiny scrap of pale blue paper.

Heart aching, I pull at the zip, tug out the note and unfold it.

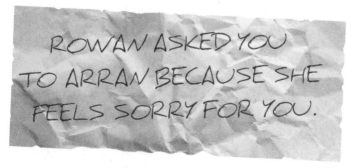

ROWAN ASKED YOU TO ARRAN BECAUSE SHE FEELS SORRY FOR YOU.

"What's up, Lil?" asks Rowan.

I scrunch up the paper; push it as far into the depths of my bag as it will go.

"It's nothing."

Proof. It can only be Georgia. She must have slipped the note into my bag in the car. Getting through this weekend is going to be even tougher than I thought.

Rowan's mum calls us to come and help set the table over in the farmhouse.

I am nervous as I place several crystal wine glasses on the huge pine table, scared I'll drop one and be asked to pay for it. Rowan puts out the cutlery, fancy cloth napkins and side plates.

"Use the napkin rings, Rowan." Her mum hands her some round wooden objects that I'd thought were bangles.

It seems a huge amount of fuss for one meal, and the strangeness of it all makes me feel homesick. Why go to the bother of pouring milk into a jug when it comes in a perfectly usable carton? And what on earth is the point of a napkin ring?

The curry is delicious, however, and I feel quite posh sipping my fizzy apple juice out of a crystal wine glass. The big farmhouse kitchen is cosy, warmed by a log-burning stove. Everyone is chatting happily and I have made sure that I'm seated between Rowan and David, as far away from Georgia and Fiona as I can get. Even though Georgia is effectively ignoring me, at least she isn't saying anything mean. Gordon tells some terrible jokes. I think he must have memorised them from last year's Christmas crackers.

But then it all goes horribly wrong.

PING!

Fiona taps her glass loudly so that everyone turns to

look at her. Then she points across the table to where I am sitting, nibbling at a piece of warm naan bread.

Suddenly, everyone's eyes are on me.

"I want to hear all about Lily!" she announces. "Tell me all about yourself, dear. Georgia's never said a word. I didn't realise you were one of her little friends."

What am I supposed to say to that? I can hardly tell her I'm not Georgia's friend, little or otherwise, and that Georgia acts like I don't exist most of the time. I can't tell her Georgia's trying to bully me by leaving nasty notes in my locker and in my bag.

"Um, we're in the same year at school," I mumble. "I've been best friends with Rowan since nursery when I fell off my trike into the sandpit. I made friends with David in P3 when we bonded over a shared horror of gymnastics."

"And a shared love of dinosaurs and zombie comics," adds David. "I have also been attempting for years to get Rowan and Lily interested in *Star Wa*—"

Fiona waves a dismissive hand. "We're already more than aware of your obsession with *Star Wars*, David. The evidence is in front of us."

She points at David's cloak. David's mum's face darkens.

Fiona turns back to me and carries on with her interrogation. "And what about your parents, Lily? Should I know them? What does your dad do?"

Georgia sniggers. "Lily's mum's a cleaner and a waitress. You met her in that pokey café, Mum. Don't you remember? You said the coffee was— ow! David, you kicked me!"

"Did I? Sorry, knee-jerk reflex... total accident," says David. "So, what's the plan for tomorrow, because if I'm going to be dragged up a mountain, I'm going to need an early night."

"Me too," says Rowan, yawning widely. "I vote the four of us watch a film in the TV room and then head for bed."

We stand up and leave the adults in the kitchen. I'm glad to escape.

By the time the movie ends, I am curled on the couch, cosily covered by a fluffy blanket, struggling to keep my eyes open. David and Rowan are on either side of me, tucking into an enormous bowl of microwave popcorn. Georgia is sprawled next to Finn on the rug, her elbows on a heather tweed cushion, her silky blonde hair flowing down her back. She has changed into a pair of tartan pyjamas and furry slippers and is flicking through a glossy magazine. She yawns loudly.

"That film was a drag. Arran is already turning out to be deadly dull. Let's liven things up with a game of truth or dare. Who wants to start? I vote Lily." She scrambles to her feet and stands in front of me, hands on her hips. "Right, Lily. What will it be... truth or dare?"

Neither, I think, but that option doesn't appear to be on offer. And I guess I should feel pleased that Georgia is including me. Still, I can't help feeling that this is going to end badly.

"I can't stand that stupid game," sighs David. "Let's just head for bed, eh?"

"So, truth or dare?" Georgia doesn't take her eyes off me. She taps her foot on the floor.

It very much depends on the question, I think. Honesty isn't always the great quality it's made out to be. Sometimes, it's much safer to keep the truth well hidden.

"Dare," I say at last, throwing off the heavy blanket.

Georgia turns towards Rowan and David. "What should we make her do?"

"Nothing energetic," laughs Rowan. "I'm far too tired for running-around-the-garden-type dares. We could dare her to creep up on the adults and make them jump?"

Dave shakes his head. "I wouldn't advise giving my mum a fright. She has lightning-quick reflexes, like my own, and might do one of her ninja kicks if she thinks Lily's an intruder. I seriously think we should just call it a night."

"*I* know what Lily can do." Georgia looks at me with an unmistakably malicious glint in her eyes.

I hold her gaze. My heart is thumping in my chest.

"I'll give you a simple one. I dare you to go down to the shore and fetch some seaweed. Easy peasy."

Rowan and David jump up so quickly that popcorn spills from the bowl. Finn leaps to his feet and gobbles them up. He's a living hoover, that dog.

"No way, Georgia," says David. "That's not fair."

"Everyone knows what happened to her in the summer," adds Rowan.

"I'm not daring her to go in the water!" laughs Georgia. "That would be dangerous, especially in the dark. The seaweed's all over the pebble beach. All Lily has to do is collect a single strand from the shore. She'll be quite safe. But if she's scared…"

"It's fine. I'm not scared of water," I insist. This is true, to an extent. I'm not one bit afraid of warm bubbly baths, sparkling blue swimming pools, trickling streams… but dark waves sloshing against a harbour wall at night time totally freak me out now. On the other hand, it suddenly seems very important to show Georgia that I am not afraid of her and her dumb dare. "Challenge accepted."

I don't listen to Rowan and David, calling me to come back.

The farm track leading to the main road seems longer and bumpier in the pitch dark. I stumble along, wishing I had brought a torch. Then I remember that my phone has a light. I use it steer round the potholes in the lane, cross the deserted road and make my way over rocks to the narrow strip of pebbly beach. I'm not scared, although I jump in the air when a black shape brushes heavily against my leg. I shine the light downwards.

"Hi, Finn. Thanks for coming." I bend down to give him a pat.

He licks my hand. His paws scrabble on the pebbles as he leads me down to the sea. Finn thinks a walk in the pitch dark is a perfectly fine idea, and for a moment I feel quite cheerful about it too.

My phone's light eventually shines on the first few strands of slippery seaweed, twining around my feet like a mass of wriggling eels. I reach down to pick up a strand and tug hard.

But as I pull, my foot slips on the tangle of seaweed and I fall. My phone skitters on the pebbles and the light dies. I am alone in the pitch black, hands clawing at different textures, clammy damp seaweed, hard pebbles, grit.

The invisible sea makes an eerie sucking sound, as if it's trying to pull me into its depths.

I try to get up, but the weed's slimy, the smooth rocks slick with seawater.

The tide's coming in, greedy waves slurping towards me.

I'm trapped, sinking in wet sand, caught in a tangle of slippery weed.

The sea's coming to get me. It'll grab me, tug me under.

I'm gasping for breath. My throat hurts.

Remember to breathe, my brain tells my body. *In through the nose: 1... 2... 3... 4. Out through the mouth: 1... 2... 3... 4.*

I had to have a few counselling sessions after the night I fell off Millport pier. I thought they were pointless – until now.

I push myself up on to my hands and knees and feel about for my phone. Mum will be raging if I've broken it. *Stupid game... Stupid Georgia... Stupid me for accepting the dare.*

The beach is suddenly bathed in light and I blink, blinded.

"Lily! Where are you, Lil!"

I have never been so glad to hear David's cheerful voice.

"Oh, there you are!" he calls towards me. "What are you doing, Lil? Why are you sitting on the beach? It's not really sunbathing weather."

"Thanks for that, Dave. Now, can you stop laughing, come over here and help me up? Finn, get off my legs, you big eejit!"

"What happened, Lil?" Rowan is there too. "Are you hurt?"

"I slipped on the stupid seaweed, but I'm ok."

I hear their feet crunching across the sand and pebbles.

"Careful!" I yell. "I dropped my phone. Don't stand on it!"

Rowan swings her torch beam round. It glints on a huge expanse of rippling black water just a few metres away from where I fell. I'm glad I couldn't see how high the tide was when I fell.

"Here it is." Rowan rescues my phone from a clump of slithery seaweed. "Is it broken?"

"It would serve me right if it was. Coming down here in the pitch dark was not one of my smartest moves, was it?"

"No, Lily. In fact, it was really dumb. I couldn't believe it when you sped off like that. By the time Dave and I fetched our torches and wellies you were long gone. We told Georgia not to bother coming, since she's in her pyjamas."

"And it was her fault in the first place," grumbles Dave, taking my arm and heaving me to my feet. "That was a really stupid dare. It was cruel of Georgia to suggest it when she knows what happened to you in the summer."

"Oh, Dave. I'm sure she didn't do it on purpose!" says Rowan. "Georgia is just a bit thoughtless sometimes. You shouldn't have yelled at her like that, Dave. She looked quite upset."

"Well if I didn't upset her, I'm sorry. I meant to." David shines his torch under his chin and grins evilly. "And Rowan, sometimes you're just *too* nice. It's a bit sick-making."

"Thanks, pal. I love you too. Finn! Come here right now! You can go for a swim in the morning, you daft dog!"

When we reach the house, Georgia is curled up on the couch, a fluffy dressing gown draped over her shoulders. She doesn't look upset at all. In fact, she looks quite pleased with herself.

I drop the soggy strand of seaweed right into her lap and she leaps up, squealing. The seaweed slithers down her leg and coils round her ankle.

"Don't!" she shrieks, kicking it away with a shudder.

"Well, you asked for that," laughs David.

"You're so childish!" Georgia flicks her hair and sits back down, pretending she hadn't been scared.

I don't know if she's speaking to me or to David.

Rowan grins mischievously. "Now it's your turn, Georgia. Truth or dare?"

For a moment Georgia looks annoyed, but then she yawns theatrically. "We can carry on the game tomorrow, maybe. I'm off to bed. Night all."

"Well, don't think we'll forget!" Rowan calls after her.

"Wow, Rowan," says David. "What happened to Miss Nicey-nice?"

"I just like things to be fair," says Rowan calmly. "And Georgia's not being fair. Let's get to bed, Lil. We've got a busy day tomorrow."

We crunch across the gravel towards the cottage: me, Finn and my best pal.

"I'm so glad you came, Lily." Rowan slips her arm through mine. "Things are always better when you're around."

Chapter 13

Reasons David's cool, despite being a geek:

- He doesn't care if other people think he's crazy.
- He always stands up for his friends.
- Even when he's moaning, he still makes us laugh.

When I wake up on Saturday morning, I slip out of bed and tiptoe to the window, trying not to wake Rowan, who is snoring gently, cheeks flushed and brown curls in a messy tangle.

I pull the flowery curtain to one side, stand for a moment and stare at the beautiful sea view.

Across the water, my sister could be about to make the biggest mistake of her life.

"Oi! Bright light! Bright light!" shrieks Rowan, tugging the duvet over her head. "Is it even morning?"

"It's half past eight," I say, glancing at her watch on the bedside table. "Your dad said we had to be up for breakfast at nine."

"Half past eight!" wails Rowan. "That's the middle of the night!"

"The sun's up," I point out. "Look at the view!"

I pull the curtain fully open so she can see the sea, misty in the distance, tinged pale apricot by the weak morning sunshine.

"Pretty," she concedes, rubbing her eyes and sitting up in bed. "Ok, you win, Lily. Let's get dressed and see what Dad's created for our breakfast. I expect it'll be eggs. Just don't be surprised if it's some weird experiment, like eggs and seaweed. My dad thinks he's Jamie Oliver."

Ten minutes later, we're in the cosy pine kitchen, twirling on the tall stools at the breakfast bar while Gordon rustles up breakfast.

Finn follows him around the kitchen floor, scoffing up crumbs in his wake.

"Are scrambled eggs ok with you, Lily?" asks Gordon, and then looks puzzled when Rowan and I start giggling. "What's so funny?"

"I told Lily you would make eggs, Dad. But what's the twist? Eggs and sprouts? Eggs and ice cream?"

Gordon looks a bit miffed for a moment, but then grins widely. "My original plan was for egg soup, but I'm going for scrambled eggs and smoked salmon instead. Boring, I know…"

I've never eaten smoked salmon before, never mind with eggs, but when we tuck in it tastes pretty good. Better than Gran's porridge, but not as good as her fry-ups.

"That was totally delicious, Mr Forrest," I say, as I take my plate over to the sink. "Thank you very much."

"No, thank *you*, Lily." He beams. "Rowan, why aren't you as well mannered and helpful as Lily? Where did your mother and I go wrong?"

Rowan groans. "I knew you'd show me up, Lil. Stop being so good all the time," she teases. "Right, let's go and drag David out of his bed. We should maybe leave Georgia to get up on her own. Fiona will freak if their beauty sleep is disturbed."

We walk across the courtyard to the big farmhouse. The door is unlatched so Rowan wanders confidently inside. I follow, feeling a bit shy, especially after the trauma of last night's dinner.

David doesn't need to be dragged out of bed. He's already up, sitting in the enormous kitchen, pulling on a pair of heavy lace-up boots. He's wearing waterproof trousers and a fleece zipper.

Rowan stops and stares. "Wow, look Lily. It's Mr Outdoor Adventurer!"

David pulls on a black beanie hat and grins at us.

"I guess you've learned your lesson after last year's debacle?" says Rowan.

David nods glumly. "Yup. Trainers do not work as well as wellies. And jeans get really cold and heavy when they're soaking wet. Now I'm ready for anything: from wolf wrestling to climbing inaccessible peaks. Bring it on."

"I'm not sure wolf wrestling is an actual thing," I say. "But you definitely look prepared for climbing. *Are* we climbing?"

I'm suddenly anxious that I might not have the right clothes with me. I have a vision of the Arran Mountain Rescue Team being interviewed on television, all of them looking stern and disapproving, as they describe how a stupid twelve-year-old girl climbed Goatfell in a fluffy cardigan and jeans, got lost in a blizzard and had to be brought down from the mountain on a stretcher.

"No, no, just walking up a hill," says Rowan. "We're going up to a lochan, which is a mini loch, high on the hillside. If you're really lucky you might even see a golden eagle. Have you brought your notebook? Your bird sketches on Millport were beautiful. I bet you end up writing *and* illustrating books about birds and wild animals when you're older."

I don't reply, but I feel my cheeks reddening and have to turn away. Rowan's compliment should have made me happy, but it only reminds me how mean I've been to Brian. She's too busy prattling on to notice my embarrassment, but David gives me a funny look.

"Are you ok, Lily?" he asks. "If you don't fancy the walk and the picnic, we could just hang around here, or walk into Brodick."

"Don't put her off, Dave, just because you're a lazy lump!" says Rowan indignantly. "I've brought two pairs of walking boots, my new Timberlands and my old ones, which are too tight for my big fat feet. They should fit you, Lily... And there's loads of waterproof clothing hanging up in the vestibule. We'll get you all kitted out for a hike up Kilimanjaro."

David's mum lumbers into the room, laden with rucksacks and waterproof jackets. She certainly looks ready for Kilimanjaro.

"Good to see that you three are up out of your beds at a decent hour!" she bellows. "David, are you wearing a thermal vest? And have you put your inhaler in your rucksack?"

"Yes, Mum, I'm wearing ample underwear, thank you. And my inhaler is in my rucksack. And you have just made me look like dork-of-the-year in front of my friends, so thanks for that."

Fiona sweeps into the room. Her hair is brushed and her make-up applied, so she has obviously been up for a while, but she stretches and yawns. I can see where Georgia gets her drama skills.

"What a dreadfully uncomfortable bed!" she says, rubbing at her neck. "I couldn't sleep a wink!"

"That's odd. I'm sure I heard you snoring through the wall," is David's mum's sharp reply.

Sometimes David's mum sounds a lot like Miss Swanage. Maybe it's because they're both gym teachers.

An hour later and we're halfway up a mountain. Well, ok, not quite. It's a hill. But it's steep and rocky with little waterfalls, a burn with stepping-stones and frequent patches of very boggy ground. The path we're following winds upwards through bracken and heather, and it's quite hard work, but also really satisfying.

When I turn my head, I can see the sea far below; ahead of me, black mountain peaks. It's wild and beautiful and I scan the sky for golden eagles.

We lead the way: Georgia, Rowan, David, Finn and me. The adults are far behind, although David's mum has the picnic in her rucksack so there's not much point in getting to the lochan before her. We've sped ahead for the glory of winning. And it does feel quite good. Miss Swanage was right about that.

"Are we nearly there?" I gasp, as we scramble over slippery granite slabs. My legs are starting to feel wobbly. Perhaps I should take more interest in P.E. after all. I'm clearly a bit unfit.

Rowan and Georgia are bounding along in front, accompanied by Finn, who is having a fine time splashing through bogs and scrabbling at rabbit holes. They have to stop to let Dave and me catch up. But David, despite being a bit overweight, is coping much better at clambering over the rocks than I am. That might just be because my borrowed boots don't fit very well – or because my worries about Jenna are weighing me down.

"Not far now," says David. "Think yourself lucky that we aren't doing this in a snowstorm or a hurricane. I've endured conditions you couldn't imagine in your worst nightmares up here."

I laugh, and we stop to catch our breath.

"Tell those two to slow down," says David, loudly enough for everyone to hear. "Or I'm going to have a major asthma attack."

"You're not even wheezing," Rowan calls behind her, rather unsympathetically. "Stop being such a baby, Dave."

"There it is!" shouts Georgia. "Coire-Fhionn Lochan. What do you think, Lily? It's a registered wild swimming site. Anyone fancy a wee swim?"

The tiny loch is beautiful, in a teardrop-shaped dip between the peaks. The water is grey silk, fringed by a white gravel beach. But, to be totally honest, I'm more impressed by the fact that Georgia has just spoken to me in a friendly, non-sarcastic tone.

"It's gorgeous," I say quietly, scared to spoil it all by saying the wrong thing, dreading that awful mocking tone returning to her voice.

"It is beautiful, but that's a freezing wind, isn't it?" Rowan zips up her red, fleece-lined jacket and draws her hat down over her ears. "And I expect the water is ice-cold. David wouldn't last two minutes in that water before he got hypothermia."

David laughs. "What do you think, girls? Should we dare Georgia to swim across the loch?"

"No way!" shrieks Georgia. "I'm going for truth, not dare!"

"I'll think up a good question later," says Rowan. "And if the picnic doesn't arrive soon, I vote we resort to cannibalism and eat Lily."

"I knew you brought me to Arran for a reason!" I laugh. "But you'll need to fatten me up first, preferably with picnic food."

The wind whistles across the water, blowing my hair into a messy tangle. I'm very glad for my waterproof jacket. It's cosy and the trailing sleeves are useful for keeping my hands warm. Finn on the other hand doesn't care about the cold. When David throws a pebble in the water, the crazy dog leaps in after it.

The adults arrive within a couple of minutes, Dave's mum striding across the path in the lead.

"Come on, come on! Keep together. No slacking!" she calls, in her best P.E. teacher voice.

I'm surprised she hasn't brought her whistle.

We spread waterproof groundsheets on the white gravel beach and flop down, hungry and exhausted. There are masses of tuna-salad sandwiches and egg-mayonnaise rolls. It's just as well there are lots, because we fall on them like a pack of ravenous wolves.

Finn sits right beside Fiona, his head on her knee, trying to look pathetic while she eats her sandwiches. Traitor.

My fingers are numb with cold and opening my packet of cheese and onion crisps is a tricky mission. So I'm excited to see Rowan handing out plastic cups of tomato soup from a gigantic flask.

"I'd comment on this soup tasting particularly delicious because we're eating outside," says Dave, "but I'm scared of sounding like one of the Famous Five."

"Yeah, you do. You sound like Anne, the wimpy one," sneers Georgia.

"Cutting." Dave grins.

He never seems bothered by Georgia's snarkiness. Maybe I should try and be more like him and laugh her comments off instead of taking them to heart? But then Dave isn't getting mean comments in writing.

We finish our picnic. I lean against a rock to digest.

"You've got a tomato-soup moustache, Dave," I tell him.

"Great," he says. "Probably the nearest I'll ever get to having facial hair."

Fiona unlaces her leather boots and pulls down her sock to show a tiny blister on one heel.

"I have blisters on my blisters," she moans. "These new boots are useless. I should have worn my trusty old pair, but I foolishly gave them away to my cleaning lady."

She looks me up and down, taking in my ill-fitting waterproofs and too big boots.

"How does your mother manage?" she says. "It must be a real struggle for her to bring up all those children alone on a cleaner's wages. No wonder you're a scruffy little thing."

I feel myself blush a fiery scarlet … so much for laughing off nasty remarks. I open my mouth to speak and then close it again, gulping like a landed fish.

Rowan is over at the waterside with Finn and Georgia, tossing gravel into the still, grey water and watching the ripples spread. But I'm sure David heard. I am cringing with embarrassment, and when I finally speak, my voice trembles.

"My mum manages ok. She has two jobs. She works hard. She—"

"Lily's not scruffy!" breaks in David, suddenly. "She's smart-casual, aren't you, Lil? Some people try too hard, if you ask me." His voice so cold that he doesn't sound like the David I know. "And those people just end up looking a bit ridiculous. Come on, Lil. I bet you can't skim stones as well as me. I am a *complete* legend."

He pulls me up, splashing the remains of my soup, and drags me over to the water's edge. He picks up a large stone and slams it into the water so hard that we have to jump back to avoid the splash. Finn goes crazy with excitement and throws himself in after the stone.

"Calm down, David," I say softly. "Keep your hair on. But lose the moustache."

David wipes away the tomato soup from his upper lip. His hand is shaking.

"No, it isn't, Lily. It's not ok at all. She called you scruffy! She's a total witch!"

"I've been called worse," I sigh.

"What do you mean?"

All this time I've tried to keep the notes a secret, but I suddenly know telling David will help. He'll always be on my side. I look over at Rowan and Georgia. We're far enough away for them not to overhear.

"Someone has been leaving nasty notes in my school locker, saying that Rowan wishes I would leave her alone and that I'm 'clingy'. They've also put a note in the bag I've brought to Arran. It says Rowan has only asked me here because she feels sorry for me."

David shakes his head angrily. "That's horrible. You *do* realise that Rowan has never said any such thing, don't you? She loves you to bits."

"I did wonder, at first, if Rowan was talking about me behind my back, but it finally dawned on me that the notes couldn't be true. I've had four so far. You're the first person I've told."

"Why didn't you tell me when you got the first one?" David actually sounds hurt. "I've watched *Sherlock*. I could have helped you track down the culprit. You shouldn't keep stuff like that to yourself, Lily."

"I know. You're right," I say. "I thought I could sort

it out myself, but keeping it quiet is just making me miserable."

"And do you know who's writing them?"

"I'm not sure enough to accuse anyone, but I have my suspicions."

He raises an eyebrow. I can tell we're both thinking the same thing. David glances along the water towards Georgia. She's still chatting and laughing with Rowan.

"It *must* be her. If there's one in your bag, how could it not be her?" He sighs. "Though it does seem a bit low-tech. I'd have had her down as more of a cyber bully. I guess it's because she feels a bit left out sometimes."

"Left out?" I can't wrap my head around the idea of Georgia as a victim.

"Yeah. Jade and Danielle have been best pals since nursery; and you, me, Rowan and Aisha are always hanging around together. Sure, Georgia likes to boss Danielle and Jade around, but she doesn't really have a best friend of her own. Danielle copies everything Georgia does, but you can tell she's mostly afraid of her. Jade is Danielle's real friend."

I haven't thought about it like that before. At school, Georgia seems to have everything: popularity, nice clothes, money. But David's right. She doesn't have a really close friend. And her mum isn't exactly the sweet, motherly type.

Perhaps Georgia does feel left out. It's a mind-blowing struggle to try to picture it from her point of view, where I'm the one being unfriendly. But what am I supposed to do when they're standing in a knot, sniggering behind their hands at me? When they're not inviting me to their parties?

"Maybe you should tell Rowan about the notes," whispers Dave, as the two girls head towards us.

"No! I don't want her to know. She would be really upset. And I can't just accuse Georgia without any proof."

"Well, when we get home, I'm going to look out my deerstalker hat and magnifying glass and find out whodunnit."

"Ok." I smile at the thought of David in a deerstalker. I feel lighter, as though a weight has just lifted from my shoulders. "You can be Sherlock and I'll be Watson. We'll solve this mystery between us."

Chapter 14

I dream of having these things when I'm older:

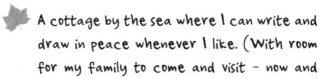

🍁 A cottage by the sea where I can write and draw in peace whenever I like. (With room for my family to come and visit – now and then, and not all at once.)

🍁 A black Labrador called Poppy.

🍁 A ragdoll kitten called Archie.

Rowan seems to have conveniently brought two of everything on this holiday. When we go swimming in the lovely pool at Auchrannie on Saturday afternoon and I pull my horrible ruffled pink costume from my bag, she suddenly remembers that she has a spare one. It's a lovely sapphire blue colour and I love it.

I love the pool too. After the climb up to Coire-Fhionn

Lochan this morning it's brilliant to luxuriate in the jacuzzi, though I'd be feeling more relaxed if I had succeeded in contacting Jenna this afternoon. We only had a couple of minutes back at the house to collect our swimming gear, and I decided to sneak upstairs and have a go at sending Jenna a message, warning her to stay away from Kai tonight. I pulled out the cushion and hugged it to my heart – just as Georgia and Rowan walked into the bedroom.

"Aw, look! Lily's brought her comfort blankie!" sneered Georgia.

"So have I," said Rowan, lifting a fluffy pink teddy from her pillow. "Splodge comes with me wherever I go. Are you ready, Lil?"

Flushing scarlet, I stuffed the cushion back in my bag.

There's nothing I can do for Jenna while I'm at the pool, so I try to enjoy the moment.

"This is the life," sighs Rowan, kicking her feet in the frothing bubbles. "When I grow up, I'm going to have a hot tub in my garden. And a bubble-gum-pink Porsche. I'm going to do useful stuff too, like find a cure for cancer and a solution to global warming."

"I'm going to be a famous actress." Georgia closes her eyes dreamily. "I'll live in a mansion in Beverly Hills in California, with a maid, a cook and a gardener – and I'll never lift a finger."

"Oh come on, Georgia! You don't exactly work your fingers to the bone at the moment." David is laughing, but there's a slight edge to his voice. "I'm going to be a film director and have a private museum of Star Wars memorabilia. What about you, Lil?"

"When I grow up, I'm going to get a dog," I say. "A big soppy black Labrador, like Finn. I'm going to call her Poppy."

"Is that it?" says Georgia, eyes incredulous. "That's all you want out of life?"

"I've got lots of dreams, Georgia, but that's a brand new one." I try to keep my voice cheerful, aware now that all this time I may have been coming across as unfriendly towards her as she has been to me. "I thought I liked cats more than dogs, but being with Finn this weekend has changed my mind. I'm going to have a ragdoll kitten as well, of course."

Georgia smiles – a proper smile, not her usual sneer. "Ragdolls are cute. They have beautiful blue eyes, haven't they."

"Oh, I nearly forgot!" says Rowan, leaning forward and splashing water lightly over Georgia. "What's it going to be? Truth or dare?"

"Oh no! I was hoping you'd forget about that!" Georgia slides under the water and rises back up, fair hair silky wet as a mermaid's, eyelashes sparkling with droplets of water. "I already chose truth, remember?"

Rowan opens her mouth to speak, but David gets in first.

"Right, answer this question truthfully." He has a wicked glint in his eye. "Have you ever sent an anonymous letter to anyone?"

"Weird question, Dave," says Rowan, frowning.

I can't believe he's just said that. And he's too far away for me to kick or nudge him in the ribs. David's approach to detective work isn't exactly subtle, but Georgia doesn't look fazed.

"That's easy." She leans back in the bubbles, kicks her painted toes. "Never in my life. If I've got a problem with someone I tell them to their face. Why wouldn't I? Anonymous letters are lame."

She stares up at the ceiling and David raises his eyebrows at me.

She's fibbing, he mouths.

I look at her and decide that David's right. Georgia looks totally at ease, which only proves that she's an excellent liar.

It's after ten o'clock on Saturday night. The night of Kai's planned break-in. I'm dead tired after our long walk, two hours in the pool and another big evening meal followed by board games, but I've got Jenna's life to save.

I lean over and switch on my phone's torch. Rowan doesn't even stir. She's sound asleep, snug under the flowery duvet. Quietly and slowly, I unzip my schoolbag and pull out the purple cushion.

I hold the cushion tightly, close my eyes and try and think of another happy memory. Like last time, I struggle to find a memory that isn't spoiled by the looming presence of my stepfather: bellowing like an angry bull because his dinner wasn't ready, or his shirt wasn't clean, or he'd just tripped over the cat.

Then, totally unexpectedly, I remember an incident I must have locked away right at the back of my mind.

It's Christmas morning, I'm seven years old. Waking up before 6 am, totally over-excited, leaping about on the furniture, trying to get everybody else out of bed.

Flash forward a couple of hours: Gran hands over Jenna's present, an art set, which she really likes, and which I immediately envy. My parcel is wrapped in beautiful gold paper with little reindeer leaping across it. Mum tries to salvage the paper, but I rip it into tiny bits. I'm anxious to see what's inside, scared that it won't be as good as Jenna's boxed rainbow of oil pastels and felt pens, terrified it'll be one of Gran's itchy knitted jumpers.

But for once, the reality is even better than anything I could have imagined. It's my favourite ever Christmas gift:

a Sylvanian horse-drawn caravan with a cute squirrel family. The squirrels are improbably dressed in old-fashioned outfits, little pinafores and trousers with braces. In the caravan are wooden drop-down beds with miniature quilts, a tiny toilet and even a little kettle for the stove. I am beside myself with joy.

Zoom forward again. Gran has settled down to watch the Queen's Speech. Mum is in the kitchen, burning the turkey. Then my step-dad comes into focus. He's been quite jolly so far, but very unsteady on his feet. I see the next bit in slow motion: he gets up from the couch to grab another can of beer from the fridge, trips over the rug and lands heavily on my Sylvanian caravan, smashing it to smithereens.

"Aw, Lil," he says, heaving himself to his feet. "I'm sorry. Total accident."

I re-live the despair I felt, picking up the shattered pieces of plastic. I know he hadn't meant to do it, and he seems genuinely sorry, but I am devastated. I cry for hours – until my big sister tells me to come and see something.

Jenna has spent the last few hours finding a shoebox, painting it bright pink and cutting a door and windows into it. The Sylvanian caravan might have been wrecked, but Jenna helps me move the surviving tiny furniture and animals into the box. I am almost as pleased with that box as I had been with the actual caravan.

I recall how, on the days I got scared or upset by my step-dad, Jenna was always there with me, holding me tightly and telling me silly stories or singing verse after verse of 'The Wheels on the Bus.' She was always trying to make my childhood better for me.

My head is swimming with these memories. Tears trickle down my cheeks. I'm dizzy, and I experience a weird falling sensation that makes my arms flail like windmills.

There's a sudden breeze, cold against my face. I open my eyes and look around, trying to work out what's going on. *Have I sleepwalked out of the cottage?*

I'm standing on rain-splattered tarmac, spot-lit in the yellow glow of a car's headlights as it rumbles straight towards me. I fling myself out of the way and fall next to another, stationary vehicle. Disorientated, I stagger to my feet and look around me.

I'm in Largs. I can't believe it's working. And I'm exactly where I need to be.

I'm crouching just outside the high school gate. Kai is standing in the playground only a few metres away from me: his grey hood up, a cigarette dangling between his thin fingers. In the neon glow of the lights, his skin looks pallid, his eyes black. The sight of him makes me shiver, but he isn't looking at me. He's arguing with my sister.

Jenna is standing near Kai, but she doesn't look one bit happy to be there. She shakes her head vigorously, shifts her weight from foot to foot. Damp tendrils of black hair slither like snakes across her pale face. I strain to hear what they're saying over the pattering of the rain.

"Don't risk it, Kai." Her voice is so small I have to step closer to hear her. "You'll have to break a window. The alarms will go off. We'll get caught."

Kai shrugs. He holds the cigarette to his lips. Tiny glowing embers float to the ground.

Gran would knock that thing right out of his hand. Tell him smoking was a disgusting, manky habit and he'll die of cancer, like her Jim. But Gran's not here to help me. I'm on my own.

"I'm doing this, with or without you," he says, throwing his fag end on the tarmac. "But if you don't keep look out, and I get caught, it'll be your doing. And I'll grass on you. Don't think I won't."

I hate the way he sneers at my big sister. It makes me want to punch him in the nose. But he's a lot bigger than me, and I've a feeling my punch wouldn't land. I'm filmy as mist, an insubstantial ghost.

Then Kai reaches into his pocket, holds something up. A short metal bar glints in his hand. Jenna notices the weapon at the same time as I do and she lets out a small, panicked whimper. She's as scared as I am. We're both totally out of our depth.

"Two minutes. Can you handle that?" Kai takes a step towards my sister. "Diarmid deserves everything he gets: I'll smash up his office, maybe take his laptop off his hands. It'll be a buzz."

"Yeah, if you're stupider than stupid," I whisper. My heart's thudding in my chest. I need a plan to save my sister, but I haven't got one.

Kai drops his cigarette by Jenna's feet, turns and runs towards the school building, swinging the metal bar. He hits the window of Mr Diarmid's office and smashes the glass. Tiny fragments skitter across the tarmac, glistening like ice.

The alarm goes off – or rather it goes on – and on, so loud it's making my ears hurt.

"Jen!" screams Kai, hoisting himself up on to the ledge. "Give me a hand up! We need to be quick!"

Jenna stands, looking utterly lost. Slowly, as though in a trance, she walks towards Kai. It jolts me into action.

"Noooooooo!!" I shriek.

I run towards her and try to clutch her sleeve, but my fingers don't connect.

"Don't you dare, Jenna McLean!" I yell. "How's a conviction for burglary going to look on your college application, huh?"

Jenna jumps about a metre in the air. She whirls round and stares, rubbing at her eyes as if she can't quite believe what she is seeing.

"Who's there?" she whispers. "Who are you? You're all fuzzy... Lily?"

I smile at my big sister, trying to calm her down like she calmed me when I was little.

"You know you're too good for this guy, Jenna. He's a creep."

"Is that you seeing ghosts again?" jeers Kai. He has managed to get through the window on his own. "You're off your head!"

Jenna stares at him for a long moment. He holds her gaze through the broken pane. The burglar alarm is still screeching and in the distance I'm sure I can hear a siren.

"You're right," she jeers back at him, her voice chilly. "I must be off my head, going out with a loser like you. You're chucked, Kai Dixon."

Kai's face, sickly yellow in the street light, turns goblin-like. He disappears into the room and begins his rampage. Jenna flinches at each crash.

"I'll tell the polis you're a thief!" Kai yells over the noise.

Jenna shakes her head, gives a bitter laugh. "You're on your own, creep."

She runs off, her boots clattering, and I follow. Suddenly she stops and whirls round.

"And by the way, Kai Dixon, your breath stinks like an ashtray!"

"Go, girl!" I shout. "You tell him!"

Jenna quickens her pace and I don't try to keep up with her as she rushes down the street towards home.

A police car spins round the opposite corner and screeches to a stop outside the school. Kai's struggling to get out of the window; his hood's caught on a jagged piece of glass. I grin as I watch two policemen get out of their car and head across the playground.

Haunting is much more fun than being haunted.

Chapter 15

How to cope when you're anxious (according to Google):

- Take deep breaths. (This is a bad idea if you're underwater.)
- Get plenty of sleep. (Really hard when you're anxious.)
- Don't catastrophise, or as I would say to Bronx and Hudson, "It's not the end of the world." (But what if it is?)

The next morning, after an enormous breakfast of bacon, sausage, eggs and French toast, Georgia, Rowan, David and I walk into Brodick. We leave Finn with the adults and race down the drive. Some of the shops along the front are closed because it's Sunday morning, but the Arran Chocolate Factory is open, much to David's delight.

"Best place on Arran." He drags me inside. "It's worth putting up with the midges and the rain for the chocolate truffles. And you get free samples!"

He isn't wrong. This shop is definitely the best place in Arran. It might be the best place in the whole world. The rich smell is mouth-wateringly delicious and the long rows of chocolates, glossily perfect in their long display cases, look scrumptious.

"I think I've died and gone to heaven," I whisper, breathing in the delicious smell of praline, soft fondant, fudge and caramel. The girl behind the counter offers me a free sample of chocolate and it tastes even better than it smells. Or maybe everything seems wonderful this morning because I've just saved my sister from a life of crime?

I haven't had to pay for anything yet and still have the money Gran gave me, so, I decide to buy something nice for Rowan's mum and dad to say thank you. Most of the boxes of chocolates are much too expensive, but, on a wire rack in a corner of the shop, I find a lovely little tin of truffles for just the right price. My brothers and sisters will have to do without. It won't kill them.

In the afternoon, much to David's disgust, we go on another healthy walk.

To my relief, Fiona doesn't come, as she and Rowan's mother have booked a spa afternoon at Auchrannie. Rowan's dad is driving them over to the resort and playing a round of golf while he's there. David's mum, who wrinkled her nose in disgust at the idea of an aromatherapy facial, has organised this expedition. She leads the way, because she's the one with the map, and we trot along behind.

We head along a gorse-lined path next to the golf course, and then over a long stretch of sandy beach. It's another glorious sunny day and the view's stunning. Brodick Castle nestles in autumnal woodlands and Goatfell towers behind.

"Oh, oh. She's heading into the woods. We're all going to be eaten by bears," says David, as his mother veers off the beach and crosses a wooden footbridge.

"If you meet a bear, stand your ground," I call. "They're fast runners and great climbers and swimmers, so there's no point trying to get away."

Georgia's right behind me. I hear a snort, and then a murmur so quiet the others won't hear.

"Little Miss Know-It-All."

My shoulders tense. What's the point of trying to be friendly when Georgia's so mean? Why should I even try? But if I snap at her, I'm going to ruin the afternoon for everyone else. Best to ignore her and pretend I haven't heard. Once we're back at school David and I will work together and prove that Georgia wrote those nasty notes. When she sends the next one, I'll keep it as evidence and show it to Rowan. Then Rowan will be furious with her, and none of us will ever speak to Georgia again.

That thought leads me to wonder if Jenna will ever speak to me again, or if she'll stay angry with me for the rest of our lives.

"Lily, look out!" yells David, but he's too late. I've been so immersed in my worries that I've stepped off the path. My boot slides on thick, oozing mud and I half-tumble, half-skid downhill towards the burn. I can't stop my descent and land, arms flailing, in the fast-flowing, freezing water. The others race down the slope towards me, but are too busy howling with laughter to be any use, and I've got to rescue myself from the shallow stream.

David's mum is well prepared for any emergency, however stupid. She pulls a foil blanket from her rucksack and wraps it round my shivering shoulders.

"Right, we'd best get you back to the house," she says briskly. "Don't want you getting a chill. Disappointing, as I'm sure you were all keen to see the Bronze Age hut. Come along everybody. Homeward bound!"

"Good work, Lil." David grins. "Bit extreme, but it did the job."

It's a long walk back, squelching in water-filled boots.

All the way back to the house, I stay right next to David, well out of earshot of Georgia and her cutting remarks. I feel utterly miserable.

But then David stops dead and grabs my arm.

"Lily! Look over there!"

In front of us, a tiny red squirrel is chasing another up the trunk of a tree. It stops on a branch and stares through black liquid eyes, tufty ears quivering. I feel a grin spread across my face.

"I've just discovered an important new fact," I whisper. "It's impossible to watch red squirrels and stay in a bad mood."

In the evening after dinner, the four of us huddle round the fire, playing cards. The adults are at the dining table, chatting and drinking wine. It's warm and cosy, but the gnawing ache of homesickness hasn't quite left me. I've had enough of being a guest in a strange house. I want to go home.

The next morning Rowan and I take Finn for a long walk along the beach. The sun's shining, but the wind of the sea nips my cheeks and my hands are freezing.

"Have you had a good time, Lil?" she asks. "It's been great having you here with us."

"Yes, it's been lovely. Arran's so beautiful, and I can't believe we saw a red squirrel! Thanks so much for asking me to come."

Rowan looks around, as if afraid we'll be overheard.

"Georgia's mum is hard work, isn't she?" she whispers. "Poor Georgia."

I open my mouth, desperate to tell a few home truths about 'Poor Georgia' but then think better of it. I'll wait until David and I have proof. Then I'll tell Rowan everything.

We're leaving the beach when we hear a car horn. Rowan's mum is waving frantically at us from the window.

"Come on, you two. We've been searching for you. The ferry leaves in half an hour!"

The crossing is much calmer on the way back. David and I stand outside, holding on to the railings, in our usual place at the front of the ferry. The sky's a brilliant blue, the sea frothy. I'm glad to be going home, but I'm also glad I came. Arran's an amazing island.

"I've been thinking," says David, "about the notes."

"Don't think too hard. You'll do your brain an injury."

"Ha, ha. Seriously though, don't you think Georgia sounded totally sincere when she said she'd never send an anonymous letter?"

"You said yourself she was fibbing. I expect Georgia's very good at lying to get herself out of trouble."

"Yes, but let's imagine she's telling the truth for a moment, shall we?" David furrows his brow. "Who else could it be? And how could Georgia get into your locker anyway?"

"Well, there are vents at the top of the lockers," I say. "It would be easy to slip a small piece of paper inside."

"And did it look like the notes had just been slipped through?"

I have to think about that one. Maybe David should be a detective after all.

"The first one I found was just there when I opened my locker. The second one was scrunched under my umbrella; I assumed I had just thrown some stuff on top of it and not seen it for a while."

"What if someone had hidden it there deliberately?"

"You were with me when we chose our locker codes, Dave. It could be you who sent me these notes." I smile as I speak. I know with a hundred per cent certainty it isn't David.

David laughs too. "It wasn't me, Lily. But listen, we probably weren't as top secret as we should have been when we chose our codes. There was a lot of chat with Aisha and Rowan about using our birthdays and favourite numbers. Don't you remember?"

A horrible suspicion is buzzing round my head, irritating as a wasp.

"Is there anything distinctive about the paper that might give us a clue?" asks David.

"It's pale blue. The sheets look as though they've been torn from a notebook," I tell him. "I threw them all away, I'm afraid. I get the Worst-Detective-Ever Award."

My eyes are fixed on the horizon. I'm trying to ignore the buzzing in my brain.

"Lily." David's voice is serious. "Aisha has a notebook with pale blue pages. It's in her school bag. I wrote my address down in it earlier this term."

I know what he's trying to say, but I'm struggling to believe it. My heart's pounding in my chest. I feel sick.

"I think it could be Aisha, Lil."

"It can't be!" I croak. "Then what about the one I found in my bag on Arran?"

"It's your schoolbag, right?" David's voice is gentle. "Had you emptied your bag completely before you repacked it for the weekend?"

I remember that the note was stuck in the zip. I could easily have missed it when I was trying to cram in the purple cushion.

"Why would she do such a horrible thing to me?" I whisper. "Why?"

But David can't give me an answer. He just puts his arm round my shoulders while I cry.

The rest of the journey is a blur. I sit quietly in the back of the car, eyes closed, pretending to snooze. My eyes are dry, but I am desperate to get home, run up to my bedroom and howl.

I want it to be Georgia who wrote the notes. That would make more sense. It can't possibly be Aisha. She likes me. We've been friends since the summer…

"Wake up, Lil!" shouts Rowan. "You're home!"

"We've exhausted the poor child with all that fresh air and exercise," says Fiona.

Maybe I'm getting a little over-sensitive but I think that makes it sound as if I normally live underground, like a Teenage Mutant Ninja Turtle.

"At least she was uncomplaining, unlike some," laughs Gordon.

I thank them all as I am dropped at my house, but I don't wait for their car to turn out of our street, before I run up the path, desperate to get inside. Mum gives me a big hug as soon as I'm in the door, but I rush upstairs, pretending to have a migraine. Within an hour or two, my head is thumping for real.

Mum brings me a cup of tea and pulls the curtains closed. "Poor you. Your dad used to get terrible headaches too. But did you have a good time overall?"

"Some parts were fun, some not so much," I whisper. "I missed you guys. Why is the house so quiet anyway? Where are the wee ones?"

"I had a late-night cleaning shift so they stayed at Gran's last night. They'll be back shortly I expect."

Poor Gran, I think. If I had money I would send her on a wee weekend's break to Arran. She could do with the peace and quiet.

A few minutes later, I'm still trying to sleep off my migraine when the door opens. Jenna comes over, and plonks herself down on my bed. She switches on the lamp and I blink in the bright light.

There's a look of real confusion in her eyes. Being haunted can do that to a person.

"Lily, was it you?" she whispers.

"Of course it's me. What are you on about?" I tug the covers over my head to avoid both the light and my sister, who might well be furious with me for interfering.

"I mean, was it you on Saturday night?"

"Nope, can't have been. I was in Arran." My voice is muffled, but I stay where I am, undercover.

"But I heard you. I saw you… I'm sure I did." She sounds totally baffled.

There's a short silence. If she starts yelling it will make

my head hurt even more. But when she speaks, her voice is quiet.

"Well, whoever it was, I owe them one."

She slips out of the room and I switch the lamp off. Despite the pain in my head and the dread about Aisha, I'm smiling. I helped my big sister.

The kids arrive home and Bronx and Hudson attempt – and fail – to play quietly. By late afternoon I feel well enough to get up, but I don't. I don't want to talk to anyone. I want to stay in my room and hide forever.

About seven o'clock, I get a text from David.

C U 2moro. It'll b ok.

I phone him back, because I need to figure out what we're going to do.

"It's simple," he says. "I'm going to ask Aisha if she sent the notes."

"We can't accuse her without better proof!" I wail. "Maybe we should wait, gather more evidence."

"Don't worry, Lily. I just need to wait for the right moment and then tackle Aisha. She'll be so shocked about being confronted that she'll admit everything. I'm sure of it."

I'm not so sure. This is real life, not an episode of

Scooby Doo, where the baddies confess as soon as they're caught. But I'm desperate for this to be over, so I don't argue. I need to find out what's going on. Not knowing is torture.

Chapter 16

Reasons I don't like surprises:

- You don't get to look forward to a surprise, or to put it on a list, because you don't know it's going to happen.
- Sometimes surprises are a disappointment. Like when you open a present and it's one of Gran's hand-knitted jumpers.
- And sometimes, like today, they're a horrible shock.

Tuesday morning drags by. My stomach's churning with nerves and I'm tempted to go to the school nurse and get myself sent home. I can hardly bear the prospect of hearing David fire accusations at Aisha, of seeing the shock and horror in Rowan's eyes as she realises what has been happening, of watching my friendship with Aisha disintegrate.

We're in the canteen when it happens. Aisha's been chattering excitedly about her weekend with her dad, and Rowan's now telling her all about our mini holiday. Rowan stops to take a bite of her tuna roll and David seizes his moment.

"Something horrible has been happening to Lily."

Rowan pauses mid-bite. Aisha goes very still.

"Someone is sending her nasty anonymous notes."

"What?" Rowan stares at him, eyes round.

"I think I've worked out who has been doing it," continues David, "but I hope I'm wrong."

Aisha's eyes drop to the table.

"Why didn't you tell me about this, Lil?" asks Rowan. "What kind of notes?"

"I thought Aisha might be able to explain," says David. "As I believe the notes were written on pages torn out of her notebook. You know the one, Aisha. Pale blue paper."

"I'd never do that to Lily!" Aisha leaps up so quickly that her chair clatters to the floor. "Never!"

Her shout echoes around the canteen. Nobody speaks.

Aisha turns to me, her face contorted with anger and distress. "He's lying, Lily! He's a liar!"

She grabs her bag and stumbles out of the canteen, leaving the three of us sitting, silent and horrified.

"What have we done?" I whisper.

"What on earth is going on?" gasps Rowan.

David explains, because I can't find any words.

"You don't know for sure it was her, David." Rowan's voice trembles. "What if you've made a terrible mistake?"

I'm thinking exactly the same thing.

The afternoon's lessons go by in a haze. My eyes are blurry with tears and my throat aches from trying not to break into sobs. When the home bell rings, I slip into the school library to avoid bumping into people at the gate. I can't face anyone.

When I finally get home, the door is opened by Mum, who gives me a quick hug and ushers me inside.

"You've got visitors." She nods towards the kitchen "They've just arrived."

Puzzled, I follow Mum. To my total shock, Aisha's brother Imran is standing by the table. He looks as boy-band handsome as ever in his school blazer, his shiny dark hair glistening with gel. But his mouth is a tight, hard line and his warm, sparkly brown eyes are sad and strained.

"Hi Lily," he says. "Sorry to take you by surprise like this, but I felt we had to come right away. Sort this out."

He stands to the side and I see Aisha sitting at our table. She looks terrible. Her eyes are swollen and her face blotchy and streaked with tears. She's wearing her jacket, but she's shivering.

"Tell her, Aisha." His voice is cold.

Aisha gazes up at me, tears brimming in her eyes.

"I wrote those notes, Lily," she whispers. "I wrote them and put them in your locker and your bag. I'm so, so sorry, Lily!"

The last part is a strangled wail.

"What notes?" asks Mum, banging the mug she was pretending to dry down on the worktop.

Imran explains. "She broke down crying as we were waiting for the ferry home, and told me what she'd done. I'm not trying to make excuses for her... please don't think that. But she has been so unhappy since Dad left and I think she thought that if she broke up you and Rowan then you would turn to her. I know it looks like the complete opposite, but actually, she was just desperate to be your best friend. I've explained to her that she has blown it and has acted like a complete idiot."

Imran will make a good lawyer, I think bitterly. He's made a good speech on Aisha's behalf, but his concern for me seems really genuine.

My mum steps forward, her normally placid face red with fury.

"I knew something was wrong with Lily. I had a horrible feeling she was being bullied by someone. But I never imagined it would be one of her friends."

Aisha doesn't speak. She can only cry quietly.

Suddenly my own anger dissolves like a sugar cube in a cup of tea. Aisha isn't the only one who has been nasty for the wrong reasons. I cringe as I recall my rudeness to Brian – just to impress my sister.

I walk over to the kitchen table, sit down beside her and put my hand over hers. She sobs and rubs her other hand into her eyes. I can't tell her it's ok, because it isn't.

"At first I believed what you wrote," I say. "I really thought Rowan was saying nasty things behind my back. You made me believe my best friend thought I was clingy and boring. Can you imagine how much that hurt? And then, when Dave and I worked out it must've been you…"

"I can't believe I did it," whispers Aisha, in such a tiny voice that I have to strain to hear her. "And not once, but several times. And then my dad came home. It was as if life suddenly went back to normal, and the crazy person I'd turned into in the last few months disappeared like a bad dream. Everything was ok again. But then I realised it wasn't ok. I hurt you. I'm a terrible person and I've ruined our friendship. I'm so sorry, Lil."

She lays her head down on the table and cries, great heaving sobs.

I squeeze her hand. "Thank you for saying sorry. It was a really dumb way of making a friend and I'm not sure I will get over it. But we can give it a try, see how it goes."

Aisha doesn't look at me, but she nods, head bent, her glossy dark hair swinging in her eyes. "I'm so sorry, Lily."

I can't think of anything else to say, so I lean across the table and give her an awkward hug. It just makes her cry even harder.

At that moment Jenna strolls into the kitchen from upstairs, her hair messy and her eyeliner smeared into black, panda circles. She has changed out of her school uniform into a tiger-striped onesie. When she sees Imran, she gives a small shriek and then tries to act casual.

"You might have told me we had visitors, Lil." She tries to subtly smooth her hair. "Hi, Imran. How's sunny Millport? Do you want a cup of tea?"

"Hi, Jenna. Nice tiger costume. Millport's good. You should come and visit sometime. But we'll skip the tea, thanks, got to catch the next ferry." He gestures towards his weeping sister.

Jenna looks from me to Aisha and then back to Imran,

a puzzled frown on her face. She turns and rushes back upstairs.

"Let's head off, Aisha," says Imran. "Mum will be wondering what's keeping us."

He helps Aisha to her feet, and puts a protective arm round her shoulders. She clings to her big brother the way Summer does to me.

I smile at them both, more bravely than I feel.

"Thank you for coming, Imran. You didn't have to do that. I'll see you at school tomorrow, Aisha."

I close the front door behind them and let out the breath I've been holding.

It's over.

Chapter 17

Reasons I love my family:

- 🍁 It would be really awkward living with them full-time if I didn't.
- 🍁 We keep each other safe. Well, my sisters and I do. My brothers are too busy being a pair of wee eejits.
- 🍁 They're mine, even though they're a mixed-up lot.

Jenna comes hurtling back down the stairs, jeans on, hair brushed.

"Oh, are they away already?" Her face falls. "Why was Imran here anyway?" she adds, trying to sound as if she's not that bothered.

"He was just bringing Aisha over to tell me something

that couldn't wait until tomorrow. And why are you so interested in Imran? I thought you were going out with Kai?"

"That loser? No way am I seeing him ever again." Jenna turns on her heels and stomps back up the stairs.

My heart does a happy dance. Then I do an actual happy dance, punching the air and twirling round our hall. My big sister has finally seen sense! I don't have to worry about Jenna any more.

My mum is still seething when I come back into the kitchen.

"That bullying little minx!" she mutters. "How dare she send you nasty notes... just wait until your gran hears about this!"

I shake my head firmly.

"Please don't tell her, Mum. She'll never let me hear the end of it. Gran holds grudges for life."

Mum stares at me for a moment, but then she smiles. "Sometimes I wonder who's the grown-up in our household." She gives me a hug. "By the way, Brian wants to take us all out for dinner tonight. I don't suppose Jenna will want to come, but I was hoping maybe you might..."

Mum's voice trails, her face doubtful.

"That would be great," I say enthusiastically, even though I feel shattered. "Where are we going?"

"Brian suggested Nardini's."

I've never been inside Nardini's café. It's fancy and Mum and Gran always say it's out of the question to take all of us kids there.

"That would be good," I say. "I'll go and ask Jenna. You never know, she might be persuaded by the prospect of ice cream."

I trot upstairs and knock at the door of Jenna's room. There's no point in winding her up by barging in uninvited.

"Go away! I'm busy!"

So I barge in, uninvited.

Jenna's sitting on her bed, looking fed up, and for a moment I think she's going to screech at me, but she doesn't. I try the tactics I use to motivate Hudson and Bronx.

"Jenna... remember Sarah's mum took you both for a birthday meal at Nardini's ages ago. Well, you're invited again! I can't believe how lucky you are, getting to go twice in one lifetime. Brian's taking us all out. Hurry up, we're leaving shortly!"

"You might be..." she laughs. "No way am I going anywhere with that bore."

Jenna isn't as easy to manipulate as my wee brothers. Knowing full well that I am pushing my luck, I sit down on the edge of her bed.

"I don't think we've been very fair to Brian," I say quietly. "Maybe we should give him a chance?"

"I know a boring old geek when I see one."

"You're not the best judge of character in the world, Jen. You thought Kai was the bee's knees…"

Jenna stares at me.

"It really was you on Saturday night, wasn't it, telling me to stay away from Kai?"

"I think that was probably your conscience talking," I say. "Breaking into the school would have been crazy."

"How do you know about what happened?" She jumps up. "If you weren't there?"

"Jenna. Forget it. It won't happen again, I promise. Are you coming to Nardini's or not?"

My sister leans across the bed and wraps both arms round me in a tight hug.

"Love you, maggot," she mutters. "I'm wearing my best jeans. Of course I'm coming to Nardini's… as long as I can have limoncello sauce on my ice cream."

We walk downstairs together and I push my luck with more chat. "Do you remember the day you took me sledging?"

Jenna looks at me sideways.

"And we fell off the sledge," I continue, "and then you showed me how to make snow angels?"

"Nope," she says, but she grins at me, and I know my big sister remembers it as clearly as I do.

At half past five we walk along the promenade towards Nardini's. All of us: the whole family, plus Brian. Jenna's trailing behind a bit in case any of her school friends spot her. Bronx and Hudson are screaming like seagulls, beside themselves with excitement. It doesn't bode well for our chances of a civilised meal, but for the first time in ages, I'm so proud to be in this family.

The waitress shows us to a large semi-circular booth. I slide along the bench so that Bronx and Hudson can squeeze in beside me. They gaze around, eyes wide.

"Look, Lily," whispers Hudson. "That man's got the biggest ice cream in the whole wide world!"

I look over and see the waiter carrying an enormous ice-cream sundae, topped with a fizzing sparkler. He places it with a flourish on a nearby table.

"Can I have one of those?" asks Bronx, squirming excitedly in his seat. "Please! Can I?"

"Absolutely not," says Mum firmly. "You can have an ice cream from the kids' menu, if you behave nicely during our meal."

"Aye," says Gran, "and if you don't behave, you can sit

outside in the car park until the rest of us are finished."

Bronx's lip wobbles. He opens his mouth, ready to yell.

"I'm going to have strawberry ice cream with chocolate sauce," I tell him. "What about you, Bronx? Do you like strawberry or chocolate sauce best?"

As always, food is the best distraction. Bronx weighs the options.

"Strawberry, please," he says. "Can I have fish fingers and chips first?"

"Certainly, you can have fish fingers. This dinner is my treat." Brian beams, then turns to me. "Lily, you're very good with small children. Do you think you might go in to teaching when you leave school?"

I shudder with horror at the prospect. Imagine spending every working day with little kids. Not just one or two, but twenty or thirty? I'd go nuts.

"Definitely not," I answer. "I still haven't really decided what I want to do. I was thinking I might like to illustrate nature books."

"Lily's brilliant at art," boasts Mum. "She likes drawing birds, don't you, Lil?"

Brian gives me a puzzled look.

"My drawings are ok," I blurt out. "But it doesn't help that I can't identify some of the birds. If you've still got that book, I'd really like to borrow it."

Gran beams at me. I spot Jenna rolling her eyes, but I ignore her.

Brian smiles and reaches into his rucksack. "The book's still in here. I haven't got round to returning it to the charity shop yet."

When our meals arrive, Brian lifts his glass of Irn-Bru in the air and proposes a toast. "Cheers, to the lovely McLean family, for making me feel so welcome."

We all lift our glasses, except Bronx, who is too busy slurping his drink through a straw.

"Cheers," says Mum. "To us, the Very Welcoming McLeans!"

She grins at Jenna and me, and gives a tiny wink.

"And welcome home to our Lily," adds Gran. "We missed you when you were away!"

We clink glasses, Summer bangs her spoon and Bronx sprays Irn-Bru across the table.

Which character are you?

Did you love *The Awkward Autumn of Lily McLean*?
Find out which character you're most like. Are you
loyal Lily, funny David or friendly Rowan?

It's your first day of high school and you don't have
the right uniform. Do you:
a) Join in if anyone laughs. It is pretty funny!
b) Die of embarrassment and hide in the toilets
   until your friends rescue you.
c) Tell everyone you're an exchange student from
   France. Speak with a fake accent all day.

You have to come up with a special event for school.
What do you suggest?
a) A charity fun-run.
b) A creative writing class.
c) A dress-as-your-favourite-film-character day.

If you were lost on a mountain without your phone, would you:

a) Use your compass and map to find your way home. You're too prepared to ever really get lost.

b) Worry a lot, yell for help, eventually stumble back to civilisation.

c) Build a den and fight some imaginary alien invaders.

You are put in charge of Bronx and Hudson for an hour. What do you do?

a) Think up some sporty challenges to keep them busy. It'll be fun too!

b) Take charge immediately, clean them up and give them a healthy snack.

c) (Reluctantly) bribe them with sweets so you can have the TV remote.

Who are you? Turn over to find out!

Did you answer:

Mostly a) You're Rowan! New friends are great, but you never forget your besties. You're confident, practical, friendly and ready for a challenge.

Mostly b) You're Lily! Your life might be a little crazy, but it's more fun that way. You're a worrier, but you're brave when you have to be. You're thoughtful, creative and a loyal friend.

Mostly c) You're David! Who wants to be normal? Life is so much more interesting when you use your imagination. You're dependable, witty, straight-talking and a good listener.